MY *christmas* ADMIRER

Also By Audrea Craig

Poetry:
Secret Feelings
Releasing the Storm

The Change Duet:
The Change for Her

MY *christmas* ADMIRER

Audrea Craig

Cover Art By Kyla Designs

This Book is Dedicated to

My amazing long lost sister Lani

And

My Christmas-loving mom

Christmas Playlist

That Christmasy Feeling by Johnny Cash & Tommy Cash

Hallelujah by Pentatonix

Last Christmas by Taylor Swift

Hard Candy Christmas by Dolly Parton

Underneath the Tree by Kelly Clarkson

Christmas Tree Farm by Taylor Swift

Kissin' In The Cold by JP Saxe & Julia Michaels

December

1st

It's a snowy day, extremely cold. Why would they make us go to school in this weather? I'd rather be home in my bed, cuddled up in my white fuzzy blanket streaming another episode of Grey's Anatomy.

Now, you would think I watch Christmas movies but I, Arianna Rose, do not like Christmas. I'll say it again before you think you misread what I said I do not like Christmas.

I do love the snow, watching our world slowly turn to white. Except for the fact that it makes us freeze. Everything else that comes with it, I despise. The decorations, the joyfulness, the gift giving, and the laughter. But especially, the Christmas Carolers.

Everyone always seems so happy, excited about the season, but I don't understand why. What's so fabulous about this time of year? It's just another holiday. Well that's how I see it.

I'm currently sitting in the library during lunch,

munching on my bag of Fritos, reading over my English homework one more time before I turn it in for the next class period. Our teacher gave us each a different book two weeks ago and we had to write a report about it. I was assigned Flowers In The Attic, a beautiful classic novel that Ihave read a hundred times. I even own the movie. I turn my head to examine my surroundings feeling I'm not alone like I assumed I was. I'm always the only person in here during lunch beside the librarian. That's why I always eat here.

Before you assume I'm a lone wolf, who doesn't have any friends, I do. Their names are Kate and Hanna, but sadly, we have different lunch periods. Our school is weird. You'd think they'd split our lunches into grade levels, but they don't. I'm not even going to bother trying to explain how they arranged our lunch because it's extremely confusing. So since I can't eat lunch with my friends, I eat here where it's peaceful. I don't even have to walk into the cafeteria to get my lunch since I pack my own everyday.

The bell rings signaling that it's time to go to our next class. I gather my belongings before walking out of the library.

"Bye Mrs. Hillary," I say to our librarian as I walk past her.

"Have a nice rest of your day, Arianna." She smiles at me, which I return.

I join the crowded hallway and make my way down the left-wing of the school. Heading towards literature, I move through the rowdy students so I'm not too late.

"Arianna!" I hear a familiar voice shout from behind me. I stop and turn around to see Kate and Hanna speed walking towards me, smiling.

"Hey guys," I cheerfully say with a smile. I let them catch up before continuing walking to class. One of the things I'm grateful for is that my two best friends are in my literature class. "Did you guys do the homework?" I ask them.

"Wait! We had homework?" Hanna panicked.

I couldn't help but laugh at her. "Yes, Mr. Anderson assigned us each a book to read and write a report about two weeks ago. It's due today," I told her.

"Crap. Let me guess, knowing my luck it's worth 50% of our grade." She groans.

"Sweet sweet Hanna, haven't you learned that Mr. Anderson is one of the toughest teachers in this school and every report he makes us write is always worth 50% of our grades," Kate tells her in a sarcastic smarty tone, with her arm on Hanna's shoulder. Hanna shoves Kate, pushing her into me. "Yes, Miss. I always get my work done the week before."

"At least I don't play video games 24/7 and forget any of my assignments. I care about my grades." Kate pushes her back.

"For your information, I do care about my grades. I always make sure I stay above a C." Hanna sticks her tongue out.

I couldn't help but laugh as the two bicker back and forth. As you can see Hanna and Kate are nothing alike.

Hanna is your average tomboy who loves spending her free time mastering every video game that's ever been made. She grew up with 3 brothers, so I'm not surprised.

Kate is your average book worm who dreams of going to Harvard. That's where her father and mother met. She wants to be an editor so she works very hard to keep her grades up. She even works on our school paper. She also has an older brother who is planning to get married next year.

Me, well I'm just your average girl. I just go with the flow and enjoy what life throws my way. I get A's and B's, and help my mother around the house since she is always working at the hospital. My father left us long ago when I was only 5.

"Okay guys, let's get inside before Mr. Anderson marks us tardy." I laughed, while tugging them into his classroom. This is going to be fun.

The bell rings and I let out a breath of relief that it's time to go home. I exit my algebra class and make my way to my locker. Hanna and Kate both had P.E for their last class of the day. So while I'm in the east wing, they have a long walk to their lockers from the gym in the west wing of the school.

I put in my locker combination and when I open the door to my locker, a red envelope falls at my feet. I bend down to pick it up and examine the red velvet envelope. On it, my name is scripted on it but it doesn't say who it's from.

Shrugging my shoulders, I put the mysterious envelope into my bag along with the assignments I was given for some of my classes for homework. I shut my locker door and start walking off to look for Hanna and Kate before going home.

I snicker at them when I see grumbling walking slowly down the hall. "Looks like you guys had an incredible time in P.E today."

"Shut up," Kate grumbled at me.

"Yeah, shut up. You're lucky that you don't have Mr. Baker," Hanna adds.

"What did he make you guys do this time?" I ask as we walk to the school doors.

"He made us run a mile in class today. Doesn't he know that we're lazy people who would rather sit on our butts all day." Hanna rants. "Not to mention he made us also do a course of exercises."

"Man, I hate him," Kate mutters.

We walk out the doors and into the cold breeze which hits our face, making me shiver. "I'll talk to you guys later, I'm going to hurry home. Bye loves," I say before running to my jeep.

I turn on the engine and wait for my car to heat up before driving home. Luckily, my house is only 15 minutes away from home so I don't have to drive long in this blizzard.

"Mom! I'm home!" I yell when I enter the nice toasty house. "Mom!" I yell again walking towards the kitchen. A yellow note on the fridge catches my eye. I roll my eyes, knowing what it was.

"Sorry, Ari. I got called into work. I left money

in the money jar for you to order take out for dinner. Love you, text me when you see this so I know you made it home safe." I read to myself.

I place the note on the counter before making my way up the stairs to my room. I toss my bag on my bed, walk over to my dresser and pull out a pair of sweatpants along with a long sleeve blue sweater. Once I changed into them, I text my mom letting her know I made it home.

I sat on my bed and pulled my bag towards me to pull my assignments out. The red envelope slides out along with them. I pick it up again, debating whether I should read it or throw it out.

Curiosity took over and I rip open the envelope. I pull the paper out, just to realize it was a Christmas card. Really? Everyone at school knows how much I hate Christmas, so why would someone put this in my locker?

The card was beautiful though. It was a forest covered in snow. I open the card, knowing I'll still toss it out. The note was scripted in red ink, similar to the velvet envelope.

Dear Arianna,

You don't know me but I know you. You're an amazing girl who deserves a world of happiness. Deserves no harm. You deserve someone who will constantly make your blue eyes shine. I know you hate Christmas but love, I'm planning to change that. You probably think that's impossible and are laughing at the idea. Well, I'm planning to prove you wrong.

*Every day I'm planning to put a mystery item in your locker
to get you to fall in love with this time of year.*

> *Yours truly,*
> *Christmas Angel*

December 2nd

After reading the card, I sat there holding it trying to figure out who could have put it in my locker. No one came to mind since I hardly spoke to anyone but Kate and Hanna. So it could honestly be anyone at our school.

I decided not to throw the card away only because it actually made me feel good inside. What the person said was so sweet even though they're apparently determined to make me fall in love with Christmas. Which won't ever in a million years happen. When I got to school, I wanted to tell Hanna and Kate about the Christmas card that was in my locker yesterday. Sadly, I wasn't able to since Kate's bus ran late and Hanna overslept. I had to wait until after the third period to finally tell them.

"That's so cute but funny at the same time. Even Hanna and I couldn't get you to love Christmas. We gave up." Kate said as we walked down the hall. I was on my way to the library while Kate and Hanna were heading to class.

I laugh thinking about how at the beginning of our friendship, Kate and Hanna tried so hard to get me into the Christmas spirit but failed. They ended up giving up when it finally clicked that no matter what, I'd never be into this holiday.

Their family would even try to get my mother and I to join them for their Christmas meal. My mother always denied their offer because she constantly had to work in the hospital during Christmas. I always deny it as well because I'd rather stay home by myself.

"Bye guys," I said to them when we got to the library.

"Bye," they say at the same time.

I walked into the library, noticing Mrs. Hillary wasn't at her desk. I make my way to the table where I eat my lunch every day, pull out the wooden chair and place my things down. I then open my lunch box to take my salad out.

Afterward, I unzip my bag to grab what my secret admirer put in my locker before I got to school this morning. I didn't tell Kate and Hanna because I wanted to see what the gift was and what they said in the card.

Yes, gift as in an actual Christmas present. I'm extremely curious about how they got that in my locker. I grabbed the card to open it when I heard the door to the library open. I looked over and saw that it was Samual Thomas.

Samual Thomas was one of the most popular kids in school. Now you'd think that since Samual is popular that he bullies everyone in school, but he doesn't. Samual is actually a decent guy that hardly ever causes trouble, but he does stick with his click of people.

It's weird seeing him in here, you'd think he would be eating lunch with his friends. My eyes follow Samual as he walks towards an empty table in the far corner of the library. When he pulls stuff out of his bag, I turn my attention back towards the card in my hand. I tore the envelope open, and the card was different this time. It was puppies playing in the snow. I smile at how precious it looks. I open the card and finally read what the mystery person wrote in the red ink.

Dear Arianna,

You may not know who I am but seeing you smile at school with your friends always warms my heart. The way your eyes shine as you laugh with them. Seeing you that way just constantly reminds me how much I don't want anything to destroy you. To cause you pain. Yesterday I told you I'm gonna make it my mission to get you to fall in love with Christmas. So today is where it begins. In the box is what you have to use from now on and you'll find out why when you open it. Today is a beautiful snowy day, what better way to spend a snowy day than to play in the snow. Can you guess what I'm leading to, love? Well dearest Arianna, you're going to make snow angels. Build a snowman and have fun. If you don't think I'll know If you do or don't, open the gift I bought for you. Also, your friends can help with this assignment.

I close the card, smiling at how ridiculous this person is. Thinking they can get me to love Christmas and to play in the snow. Very comical.

Yes, I love snow but I don't play in the snow. Why don't I play in the snow? Because snow angels, snowmen, snowball fights, and sledding are all a part of the holiday spirit.

I place the card down and bring the shiny gold gift in front of me. Tapping my fingers on the gift, debating if I should open it. My curiosity takes over again, wondering what my secret admirer has wrapped under the shiny wrapping paper.

Tearing open the gift, all I see is a small square brown box that I have to open. When I open the box, my smile grew bigger. Inside was a mini blue Polaroid camera. My favorite color. There was also film to go with it and a small box of chocolates.

I haven't received a Christmas gift since my father left. Yes, I receive money from my grandparents, but I never got an actual gift. My mother just gives me a gift card. Nothing special.

Kate and Hanna always tried to hand me gifts but I would never accept them. Now the only thing they give me is a Starbucks peppermint mocha. A girl can never turn down coffee. When I picked the camera up out of the box, I saw a red folded note on the bottom of the box.

Arianna,

I hope you love the gift I got you. Even though it's a gift, you'll have to use it on this Christmas journey. So today while you're playing in the snow, you'll have to take pictures with the camera so you can prove you finish the assignment. Now, you're wondering how I'll see the photos of you snow fun. Easy, hang the photos in your locker. No, I'm not a creeper. I won't take them. I'll just look at them and put you on your next mission.

Have fun xoxo

I rolled my eyes and just went back to smiling at the beautiful camera. My first actual Christmas gift.

"So you're telling me that this mystery person wants you to take pictures of yourself playing in the snow?" Kate questions as we're on my back porch.

"Yes, I said it like a thousand times," I told her.

"And you're actually going do it?!" Hanna shockingly asks.

"Yes, now can we get on with it please," I groan. I'm only doing this because the person spent a lot of money on the camera. So I figured this would be a good way to give back. Especially since there is no way I can return the gift as well.

Kate and Hanna eagerly smile and nod their heads. Of course they're excited, this is the first time we play in the snow together.

They both ran out into my yard, Hanna holding my camera. "Come on Ari, you have to take photos of you playing," Hanna teases.

I walk off my porch, into the snow. Feeling awkward at what I should do. My head turns towards Kate, laying on the ground creating a snow angel. I smile softly to myself and lay next to her so I can create my own. I close my eyes and softly move my arms along with my legs back and forth, I hear Hanna giggle to herself while she takes the photo.

"Okay, time to build a snowman," Hanna cheers. This is going to be a long night.

Thanks, Secret Admirer.

December
3rd

Snow is pretty but snow makes you cold and wet. Why did I play in the snow? Yes, it was fun. Yes, I did it because my secret admirer bought me an expensive camera. Yesterday was my first and last day of playing in the snow.

When I got to school, I hung the polaroids on the inside of my locker just like my Christmas angel told me to do, to prove that I did indeed play in the snow.

Now I'm sitting in US history, staring out the window watching the snowfall. My mind wanders to my secret admirer. Today is Wednesday, so I'm wondering how this person is planning to give me my gifts on the weekend or if they'll wait till Monday.

I hate history. It's the lamest class ever created. What is the point in learning about the history of our country, when it's all history? They tell us to focus on the future, not the past, so why are we learning about our country's past?

The bell goes off signaling that I can finally eat lunch. I grab my bag and shove my notebook inside before walking out of the room. I maze my way through the crowd to get to my locker and put the combination in. The familiar red envelope stares back at me once I open it. A smile creeps onto my face, anxious to see what my admirer has in store for me today.

"Hi Arianna," I hear Kate say walking towards me along with Hanna. I place the card inside my bag and grab my lunch.

"Hey guys," I turn to face them, shutting my locker. "You guys look extremely happy. Did you guys do something?" I raise a brow at them as we walk down the hall.

"We have a sub in our next class!" Hanna cheers.

"What class do you guys have again?"

"Chemistry," Kate answers.

"Gross, well have fun. Bye." I say before walking into the library and taking my normal seat. I place my thing on the table before pulling out the envelope. The card has a red barn with horses on it this time. One thing I like about the cards was that they weren't so Christmasy. They were pretty much nature and snow. What I love.

I open the card to read the familiar red ink.

Dear Arianna,

I hope you had fun playing in the snow, now don't worry today I'm not going to have you freeze yourself. This time I'm going to have something that'll help you stay warm. What will that be? The best thing to drink during this magical time of year. Santa's favorite drink. Hot delicious chocolate. After school, you'll have to drive safely to the best café that serves the greatest hot chocolate in town. Holly Noelle's Sweet Cafe. All you have to do is go up to the lady at the register, tell her your name and she'll give you the best drink you'll ever taste. It's on me, love.

Truly yours,
Christmas Angel

Hot chocolate, that's not too bad. I don't see how that's going to get me to love Christmas though.

The school day went by fast, I haven't told Kate or Hanna about the card yet.

I pulled into the café parking lot and parked my Jeep. I reached over the console, grabbed my wallet out of my bag, along with my camera and placed my beanie back onto my head before exiting the vehicle.

The snow stopped falling and it wasn't that windy out now. My boots sank into the snow as I walked to the entrance of the café. The outside had lights hanging on the windows, around the door, and even on the roof.

When I entered the café there was a Christmas tree in the middle of the place and snowflakes hanging from the ceiling. There was also a fireplace with stockings hung on it. The employees were even dressed up as elves.

"Okay, now I understand why they had me come here.." I say to myself.

I walked up to the lady behind the register. "Hi, what can I get you today?" She asks cheerfully with a smile on her face.

"Um, hi. I was told by someone to tell you that I'm Arianna Rose," I tell her awkwardly.

"Oh, yes. Take a seat and we'll bring you the hot chocolate." She tells me with a smile. I nodded my head and looked around to find a free table to take a seat.

I take a seat by the fireplace, pulled my phone out and waited patiently for my drink. I scrolled through Instagram and liked a few of my classmates' posts.

"Here you go, enjoy." The lady says as she places the mug in front of me. I place my phone back on the table and hold the mug in my hands.

The mug was a snowman cup, had a lot of whipped cream and candy cane in it. Along with chocolate shavings on top. I take a sip of the drink and moan a little bit at the satisfaction of it running down my throat.

I hear someone chuckle in front of me and so I place the mug down on the table and look up to see who the person was.

Samual Thomas. First the library, and now he's at this café, but this time he's actually standing in front of me. "H-hi," I say nervously, I grabbed the napkin and wiped my mouth.

"Hey, is this seat taken?" He refers to the seat sitting across from me.

"Um, no," I smile at him. Samual sits down with his drink.

"I never suspected to see you here," He lets out a chuckle.

"I heard this place has the best Hot Chocolate, so I figured to try it out," I tell him, which wasn't really a lie.

"Yeah, that's why I come here every day after school when I don't have football practice." He smiles. "That and because my aunt works here," Samual adds.

"Wait, your aunt works here?" I questioned.

"Well, she owns the place." He shrugs.

I picked my mug up and took a sip but stopped when I remembered I had to take a picture of me drinking my hot chocolate. "Um, Samual can I ask you for a favor?" I look up at him shyly.

"Sure."

I picked my polaroid up, handed out for him to use. "Can you take a picture of me drinking the hot chocolate?" I smiled at him.

"Okay," He laughs. I raised the mug to my mouth and took a sip as he took the picture. "Why did you want me to do that?" He raises a brow at me.

"It's a long story," I chuckled while stirring the candy cane around.

Samual leans back in his seat, crossing his arms over his chest. "I have time," He tells me with a smirk.

"Um, okay," I say nervously. I explained to him the whole story about how I have a secret admirer having me take pictures of myself doing every Christmas related activity to have me fall in love with the holiday. That today is just day two of the journey and yesterday the person had me play in the snow.

"That sounds extremely fun," Samual responded.

"Yeah, if you love this time of year," I tell him.

"Why do you hate Christmas?" He asked me.

I push my seat back and gather my things. "Um, that's a story for another day. I have to go." I say before getting up.

I walked towards the exit until I heard Samual call out to me. I look back towards him, just to see him following me. "Can I have your number?" He asks as he hands me his phone.

I don't say anything, I take his phone and put my number in and hand it back. "Bye Samual," I smile at him then turn back around to head home.

Task two done, what does my admirer have plan for me tomorrow?

December 4th

"Who do you think is your admirer?" Kate asks me as she munches on my chips. Her and Hanna have a substitute during their 4th period, so they magically found a way to convince him to let them do their work in the library so they can be with me while I eat my lunch. I don't know how but somehow this semester, Kate and Hanna have almost every single class together, which I'm very jealous of.

"I have no clue," I tell her before taking another bite of my salad. "Honestly, it can be anyone."

"What about Andrew?" Hanna joins into the conversation. "I heard he had a crush on you last year."

"He has a girlfriend, Hanna," I reminded her.

"Oh, that's right," She laughs.

"Maybe it's Derek," Kate suggested.

"Yeah, maybe." I take a sip of my water. "But I don't think he's the type of guy who would do this," I tell them.

"You know, it could be Samual," Hanna smirks while looking towards the entrance of the Library.

My eyes wander over to that direction, curious on why she is smirking. Samual just walked in. This is the second time he came in here during lunch. I remove my eyes from him and direct them back towards my salad. "It's definitely not Samual," I tell her.

"How do you know?" She questions.

I raised my head and looked up to where he was seated. "I just doubt that it would be him," I say. "Plus I don't want it to be him," I add before taking a bite of the greens on my fork.

"Who do you want it to be?" Kate raises a brow at me.

"Yeah, who do you want your secret admirer to be?" Hanna said in a girly high pitch tone, making us laugh.

"I'm not telling you guys," I finally say after calming myself down.

"Come on Ari, tell us," Hanna begs.

"No, remember last time I told you guys my crush?"

They both start laughing at the memory from 8th grade, where they tried fixing me up with some guy named Chris. They scared him and freaked him out, which embarrassed me to the point I faked being sick for a whole week of school.

"We were only trying to help," Kate laughed.

"By threatening him?"

"It's not our fault he couldn't take the heat," Hanna shrugs. I just rolled my eyes and continued eating my food.

"Did you get a letter today?" Kate asks.

"Yeah but I haven't read it yet," I answer.

"Well read it!" Hanna practically yells.

I reach into my bag and pull the red envelope out to read the card that's inside. I rip the envelope open and pull the card out that has a beautiful picture of a red bridge over a river with snow around it. I open the card to read the familiar red ink.

Dear Arianna,

I hope you enjoyed the delicious Hot Chocolate yesterday and agree with me about it being the best in town. Holly Noelle Sweet Cafe has always been my favorite place for hot chocolate and many other sweets. Today I'm going to have you do something I think you'll love to do. Ice skating under the Christmas lights. It's such a magical thing that I'm pretty sure will light up your eyes. So I hope you enjoy it.

> *Yours Truly,*
> *Christmas Angel*

"They want me to go ice skating today." I groan. Hanna and Kate start giggling while I lay my head on the table.

"Arianna, it's not going to be horrible." Kate laughs out.

"Guys there is a reason why I don't skate. Not only because it's something people do during this time of year. I also don't do it because I can't skate." I tell them when I raise my head up to prop them on my hands.

"It's easy, we'll teach you." Hanna smiles as she slings her arm around Kate.

"Yeah, so easy," I mumbled sarcastically when my bottom landed on the ice. As soon as Kate and Hanna got their skates, they took off without me. Even though they said they would teach me how to skate. I love having friends.

"You need help?" A stranger asks me standing in front of me. I looked up to meet the familiar brown eyes from my Algebra class. He was holding his hands out for me to grab.

"Um, yeah." My face slowly turns pink, due to the fact that I was so embarrassed that he saw me fall. I take a hold of his hands, he gently pulls me up so we both won't slip and fall onto the hard ice. "How's your bottom?" Colby asks.

"A little sore but okay," I laugh.

"I never suspected you to be a skater," He tells me.

"I'm not, I'm horrible at it. As you saw," I gesture to where I fell.

I looked towards him to see that he was smiling at me. There was humor in his eyes. I knew it was because of me.

"I can teach you," He says to me.

"N-no no, you don't have to." I stuttered. Why

am I nervous? Maybe because I just fell on my butt and didn't want to bruise another part of my body. I just wanted to get off the ice and go home.

"Yeah, I'm sort of a pro on the ice." He brags a little which makes me laugh. "Plus you won't go anywhere if you keep falling," he jokes.

"Hey!" I defensively yelled and punched his arm, which just makes him laugh. I couldn't help but giggle as well.

"Okay, lead the way," I grab a hold of his arm to use as support while he tells me what to do. I looked off in the distance to see Hanna and Kate skating around.

Kate looks my way and nudges Hanna to get her attention. They both giggle and say something to one another. Hanna lifts my camera up, takes a picture of Colby and I skating.

"How are you so good at this?" I looked up at him.

He looks down at me, smiling before looking ahead. "I come here every year during this time of year. It's a tradition for my family and I," he explains.

"So your family is here as well?" I question.

"Yeah, my little brother begged my parents to take him to get hot chocolate. I stayed back." I nodded my head and looked around the skating rink. This place was beautiful with lights hanging around it. There was also a Christmas tree in the middle of the rink with fake presents underneath.

I can see why people come here and why my secret admirer sent me here.

December 5th

Last night was amazing. I know that's shocking to hear, and I'm not saying that I'm actually falling for this holiday. I just found it fun to skate around with my friends.

We took pictures of us skating around the ice rink, even a few with Colby. Afterward, we got hot chocolate at a local stand near the area.

Kate and Hanna added Colby to the list of suspects who my admirer could be. If it's Colby I honestly don't mind but I'm keeping the window wide open. Where's the fun if you shut it down as soon as the games begin?

Lunchtime arrived, and Kate and Hanna had a substitute again which means they're back to steal my food.

"What are you doing?" I asked Kate who's making a very decorated list full of guy names.

"As you can see here," She begins talking in a very proper voice while holding the list up. "We are listing every boy in the school who could possibly be a suspect. From junior to senior." She told us.

"Okay, why?" I raise a brow at her.

"Obviously to find out who your admirer is, duh," Hanna states.

"I seriously feel like you guys are having more fun with this than I am," I told them.

"Because you're Miss. Scrooge," Kate jokes, causing us to giggle.

"We've been known," I said right before biting my apple.

I decided to open my bag and pull out the red envelope to read the card. I admire the glittery ice rink on the cover before opening it up to the red ink.

Dear Arianna,

I hope I was right about you loving ice skating. It makes me happy seeing you going through each task, by seeing I mean from looking at the photos hanging in your locker. Today's task will last you until Monday which means, I won't have any assignments for you this weekend. So this assignment is to create your very own Christmas cards for your homeroom. Trust me I'll know if you do this task or not. Have an amazing weekend.

> *Yours Truly*
> *Christmas Angel*

"Does that mean he's in your homeroom?" Kate asks.

"I don't know, maybe," I say in a confused tone. If he is, then that means there is a slim chance it's who I want it to be.

❄

"How much stuff do we need?" I asked Hanna and Kate as we walked down the craft section of the store.

"Arianna, you have a lot of people in your home-room, which means we'll need a lot of material," Kate states.

"But how do you know what we'll need?" I question.

Hanna turns to face me, holds her phone up for me to see. "I looked up card ideas on Pinterest," She smiles.

I rest my arms on the shopping cart, waiting patiently to leave this place so I can lay in my bed. When school ended, we immediately met up at the store to get everything we need to make these cards.

I'm not a craft person. I'm horrible at craft stuff, which is why art is one of my least favorite classes. So I'm grateful to have my best friends help me out on this assignment.

"Okay, we can check out now," Kate tells me. I push the cart down the aisle and start making my way to the front of the store. Hanna and Kate, were bickering about something random behind me.

I couldn't help but laugh at the two of them. No matter where we go, they always find something to bicker about. They're like two little kids.

My feet immediately glue in place, when the candy section comes to view. What can I say, you can never pass up the opportunity to get sweets.

I walk away from the cart, scanning the section to find my favorite treat. "Ugh," I say when I accidentally bump into someone. "I'm so sorry, I wasn't paying attention," I tell them before raising my eyes at the person.

"It's totally okay, I wasn't paying attention as well," Justin tells me. "Hi, Arianna," He smiles down at me.

"Hi," I shyly say back. "Um, have you seen the box of chocolate covered cookie dough?" I ask him while returning my eyes through the candy section.

"Actually, yeah," My eyes beam with excitement and look up at him. He scratches the back of his neck before he speaks again. "I sort of took the last box," My excitement fell into a frown.

"Oh, okay," I say before I start walking back to my friends.

"Arianna," I heard him say my name, I stopped and looked back at him to see him walking towards me. "You can have it," Justin holds the box towards me.

"Really?" I exclaimed.

"Yeah, I didn't really want it anyway," He tells me.

I took the box from Justin and gave him a hug, "Thank you," I say before walking to meet up with my friends.

"You're welcome," I hear say from behind me.

I smile down at the box, excited to munch on the

candy inside when I get home.

"You ready?" Hanna asks me when I catch up with them.

"Yeah, let's go." I smiled.

December 6th

Last night, Hanna and Kate helped me start making some of the Christmas cards which mainly consisted of me writing everyone's name on a piece of paper and us making a giant mess in my room.

Overall, we made only 10 cards so we had to make 8 later. We also discussed who the secret admirer could be. If the person is in my homeroom, they could be at least one of the seven guys in my class. They also feel that maybe it's not someone in my homeroom and the person is trying to throw me off. I just hope that's not true.

I've been in my room all morning, bored. I'm attempting to finish up the rest of the cards that I have to create. Each one is different from the other, but they all say 'Merry Christmas' and 'From Arianna' on them.

When the clock strikes one, my stomach begins to rumble. I make my way down the stairs and enter the quiet kitchen, searching through the cabinets, pantry, and fridge looking for something to eat since I skipped breakfast. When I shut the fridge a twenty catches my eyes along with a note from my mother.

'Here's money to get yourself some pizza, sorry I haven't gone grocery shopping yet.

See you tonight, love you'

I grabbed my phone from my back pocket to order myself a meat lovers pizza. When I got off the phone with the employee, I heard someone knocking on my door. I knew it wasn't Kate or Hanna because they always come waltzing into my place like it was their own.

When I opened my front door there was no one there, as I began to shut the door, a small box at my door caught my eye. I picked it up and walked over to the living room.

Before opening the gift I made myself comfortable on the couch and admired the silver wrapping paper with snowflakes on it. I opened the tag to see who left the mystery gift on my porch but all it said was 'Christmas Angel.' I wasn't surprised.

I tear apart the wrapping paper, just to find a velvet square box. I lift the lid up and see a beautiful silver necklace that has a rhinestone snowflake as a pendant. Under the chain was a folded little note. I gently lift the chain out of the box and grab the note underneath.

Arianna,

I smile at the beautiful necklace as I place it around my neck, I hear the doorbell ring notifying me my pizza is here.

First the camera and now this necklace, I feel guilty about the gifts, someone I don't know is spending on me and there's no way for me to thank them or give them something in return. I don't like Christmas but I don't want to get rid of these gifts. Besides this necklace, I'm very curious and a little concerned about how my admirer knows where I live.

December
7th

"Your girls are here!" Hanna announces walking into the living room where I'm on the couch cuddling a blanket. "This was taped on your door," She hands me the familiar red velvet envelope. Kate sits next to me while Hanna takes a seat on the LoveSac.

I sit up on the couch and open the envelope then slide the glittery card out. It had 4 white trees with white dots surrounding them resembling snow. Another beautiful card to add to the collection in my nightstand drawer.

Arianna,

I really hope you love the necklace. I'm gonna be honest, my mother helped me pick it out. Now today's task is something I know you never do for this holiday season. Today, you're going to decorate your house. I'm pretty sure your two besties will be really helpful for this task. Remember to take pictures.

"Ooo this is going to be fun!" Kate cheers after I finish reading the card to them. I just groan in response. My mother and I haven't decorated the house since my dad left us, mainly because we never had time to since my mother had to pick up more hours to keep the roof over our heads and food in the fridge.

"Wait! What necklace?" Hanna raises a brow at me. My fingers go up to where the snowflake pendant is laying below my neck causing her eyes to lock onto it.

Kate comes up to me, examining the pendant between her two fingers. "This is so cute, it must have cost more than my allowance."

Hanna gets up and takes a look at the necklace hanging around my necklace. "I saw this necklace at the mall when I helped my mom shop for my sister-in-law. This necklace is definitely not cheap."

I look down at the snowflake necklace and watch it glimmer underneath the light. "There's no way that the mystery person bought me an extremely expensive necklace," I say in shock. Why would this unknown person spend this much money on me? First a camera, now a necklace. What's next, a car?

Hanna and Kate grab their stuff and start walking towards the door. "Where are the two of you going?" I raise my brow at them.

"Correction three of us," Kate holds my bag out to me.

"Yeah, we need decorations and we highly doubt your mother has any hidden somewhere in this place,"

Hanna tells me while looking around the bare living room. I groan and got off of the comfy couch, went to the front door taking my coat off the coat rack, and took my purse from Kate.

Kate and Hanna have been dragging me around Target for all sorts of decorations. I keep questioning why I'm doing this but it's kinda fun to hang out with my friends and not spend most of our time sitting around watching TV. By the time we get back to my lovely home, all three of us are carrying heavy bags of things that Kate tossed into the cart.

"Okay, we're all going to be in charge of certain parts of the house," Hanna tells us when we get inside. "Kate, you're in charge of the living room," Kate gathers the bags she needs and goes into the living room. "Ari, you'll do the staircase and the entryway," I nod my head. "And I'll decorate the kitchen and dining room."

"So um, how the heck do I decorate the stairs?" I ask both of them.

"Wrap some lights and garland around the rails," Kate instructs.

'Okay,' I mouth while bending down to dig through the bags to get what I need. I grabbed the green garland and began wrapping it around the railing starting with the beam. Afterward, I plug a string of white lights and repeat what I did with the garland. "How's that?" I step back and look over at Kate, who is placing a garland along the fireplace. The same fireplace that we have never used since my mother and I agreed that it's not smart for us to attempt to try to light a fire, so we use heaters to keep us warm.

"That's so beautiful," She walks over to examine my work.

"What should I do for the entryway?"

"Now, now, you have to figure that out yourself," She smirks before going back to decorating.

I look through all the items we bought and nibble on my lower lip contemplating what I should do. Sliding my phone out of my back pocket, I open up Pinterest to find inspiration. My eyes glance at the wreath that has fake snow all over it, I pick it up along with the wreath holder on the door. As soon as I open the front door, the cold winter breeze hits my bare arms while hanging up the wreath.

Closing the door behind me, I enter back into the house and rub my arms to warm them back up. I grab the small fake tree that has led light and set it by the door. Feeling like the simple touches were good enough, I decided to check out Hanna and Kate's work. I walk towards the dining room to see how amazing Hanna transformed this place. A red and black plaid table runner across the dining table, three small trees placed along it with two candlesticks on each end. White snow-like wreaths hang on the wooden window frame.

A garland with lights hangs around the entrance of the kitchen with red ribbon bows placed on the cabinets. She placed Christmas mugs at my mother's coffee station, adding candy canes in a white jar and a hot chocolate box and hung Christmas dish towels on the oven door.

"How do you like it?" Hanna smiles proudly at her work.

"It's cute and not so crazy like I thought you would do," I laugh.

"Well, I didn't want to push any buttons since I didn't know how your mother would react." I nod my head understanding what she means. We didn't exactly ask or inform my mother about what we were doing. "Let's see what Kate did," She links our arms together and makes our way to the living room.

Two Christmas blankets were thrown on each end of the couch and another lay on the LoveSac. Festive pillows sat in front of each cushion of the couch, and a tray lay on the coffee table with candles and snow-covered pine cones surrounding them. A garland sat on top of the fireplace and four stockings hung down from it.

"Why are there four stockings? Only my mother and I live here," I question Kate.

She runs over to Hanna's side, "Hello," She laughs and points between the two of them, "Did you forget about us."

I laugh softly, "Of course." I say it was so obvious.

"Okay, we take pictures for the mystery boy," Hanna tells us while going to grab my camera.

I haven't heard anything from my mother about the house being decorated. She came home late while I was asleep and she wasn't up when I left for school. I'm cautiously waiting for a text from my mother to demand me to take down all the Christmas decorations when I get home. I let out a breath while turning the knob of my lock to open my locker. I set my belongings inside, grab the tape to hang up the pictures Hanna took of me posing around the house by our creations. One was a picture of Kate and I snuggled under a snowflake blanket on the couch, another Hanna and I were sitting on the staircase smiling while holding adorable mugs with hot chocolate inside.

Even though I'm not big on Christmas, this silly experience is helping me create fun memories with my friends. I grab everything I need for my classes along with the homemade cards Hanna, Kate and I worked hard on. I shut my locker and begin walking down the hall to my homeroom, hoping to be there before any of my classmates show up. I think it'll be awkward if someone was there watching me. Heck, when everyone sees the cards, I'll still feel awkward and embarrassed.

My feet stop in place right in front of my homeroom, I glance around the room and relief washes through me when no one is inside. I go to each desk, placing each card on the right owner's spot. This is probably the only time I'm thankful that our teacher gave us assigned seats. And that my seat is in the back so that I won't have anyone staring at me during the class period.

When I place the final card down, which is next to my seat. I sit down just when the warning bell goes off. I pull out a novel from my bag to keep my focus on reading and not my classmates taking their seats.

"Did anyone act in a way that screamed secret admirer?" Kate asked me while looking over the list of all the guys in my homeroom.

"How would I know how a secret admirer would behave?" I raised a brow at her and took a bite of an apple. We're in the library which became our new hang out spot during my lunch break. Apparently, Hanna and Kate's teacher has a sub because they're having a baby.

Kate shrugs her shoulder. "Well, have you even tried to figure out who he is?" Hanna questions.

"No, because I don't really want to know right now," Right when I said that, Samuel walks through the library doors and walks to his usual spot.

"I wonder why he keeps coming in here," Hanna said what we're all thinking.

"Go over and find out," I instruct her. She nods her head, gets up out her seat, and walks over to him.

While she investigates, I grab the red velvet envelope out of my bag and gently open it to remove the card. On the cover is a snowman wearing gloves, a scarf, and a hat, with it's arms spread wide while looking up at the sky. Around him, snowflakes fall, with the word 'believe' written in gold. I open the card to read the familiar red ink.

Dearest Arianna

,

Hope you and your best friends enjoyed decorating your home for Christmas. I know my family and I always have fun transforming our home for this time of year. Now the biggest star of each home that's decorated for Christmas is the tree. So today's task is to find the perfect tree and decorate it. Don't forget the star to top it off ;).

Yours Truly,
Christmas Angel

"So what is today's task?" Kate asks me when I set the card down

"We have to get a tree," I grumble. Kate bites her lower lip to hold back her laughter. "Shut up."

"I didn't say anything," She lets out a giggle. I roll my eyes and lean back in my seat, crossing my arms.

"What do you think they're talking about?"

Kate looks over at the two who are smiling at each other. "I have no clue."

Hanna finally gets up and walks back over to us, with a smile stuck on her face. "So what did you find out?" I lean over, propping my elbows on the table to rest my head on my hands.

"Oh, um," She pauses for a second. "He asked me out on a date. So Arianna, what's going on after school?" She tries to change the subject.

"He asked you out? So that must mean he's definitely not the admirer." Kate informs us, crossing his name off the suspects' list.

"Indeed because he's taking me out to eat this weekend," Hanna blushes.

The bell goes off, causing us to pack up our things to go to our next class.

"I still think we should get a real tree," Kate grumbles while pushing the shopping cart.

"Yeah, and I told you that my mother most likely won't be happy if pine needles are all over the floor," I tell her.

We continue walking around the store until we get to the back where all the fake trees are located. My eyes scan at all the trees that are displayed. Pink, white, purple, blue, so many different colors of trees. "All I'm gonna say is that the tree we're gonna get is going to be green," I inform them both.

I'm honestly surprised my mother hasn't said anything yet, especially since I've been using the credit card she gave me. It's basically for her to easily give me allowance since she rarely has cash on her. She also adds money when she has to travel for work. I hardly use it so I know there's a lot on the card. I also know when I spend over a certain amount it notifies my mother.

"What size tree should we get?" Hanna asks while scanning the boxes.

"That's a good question," I laugh. "We should have definitely measured the room."

"Your living room is the same size as mine, so we can get the tree size that my parents got," Kate tells me.

"Okay, well you find the right tree size and I guess I'll go find ornaments," I inform her before walking off.

Honestly, I don't know what theme to do but I feel red and white will do. I went down an aisle fill with box ornaments hoping to find something that'll catch my eyes. Just to discover there was one container filled with red, white, and silver ornaments on the very top shelf. I jump, trying to reach it but failing at each attempt.

"Need any help?" A familiar voice said behind, startling me. I turn to face them, holding my chest to calm my heartbeat.

"Um, yeah," I nervously laugh. "Do you mind?" I point to the container showing Colby what I was trying to get.

"Do I want to know why Ms. Scrooge is trying to get a thing of Christmas ornaments?" He chuckles while walking over to me to grab them off the shelf.

"It's a long story," I respond while he hands them to me.

"I have nowhere to be, so please entertain me," I shook my head while smiling and decided to share this weird Christmas admirer to him while walking to get Christmas lights. He asked me questions, like why am I going along with it, if I had any ideas who the person could be, and why I haven't informed someone that a person breaks into my locker.

That one I never thought about doing but where's the fun if I snitched on the person?

"I'm pretty sure the person doing this would make it obvious who they are," He comments while handing me a box of white lights.

"What makes you think that?"

"Well for starters, they like you so they want your attention. You said the card is handwritten, if they didn't want to be caught the person would type it out. They're giving you gifts. They also know you won't try hard to discover who they are so of course, they'll give you hints because you won't catch on or think anything of it."

"That is true but I don't think they want me to know until the days are up."

We continue walking around, Colby helping me find items for the tree and talking to me about how his family decorates and how his brother always sneaks the candy canes off the tree. After they are done, they'll drink hot chocolate while watching the Polar Express. "Here," He hands me a star. "Can't forget the star to top it off." He winks at me. "Have fun Arianna," He kisses my cheek before walking off.

I can't help but blush while staring down at the beautiful star he gave me.

"Are you done?" Hanna's voice breaks my trance.

"Um, yeah," I place everything in the cart. "I think I got everything we need."

"Okay, let's go check out." Kate pushes the cart towards the front of the store, Hanna follows behind while I stay put placing my hand where Colby kissed me.

December 9th

"Okay, my money is definitely on Colby," Hanna tells us while she tosses popcorn in her mouth.

"Same," Kate points towards Hanna before writing something down in her notebook.

"It's not Colby," I say while sitting down on the couch. We just got back from school, so now we're hanging out in my living room. The three of us planned to do homework but here we are, back to discussing the mystery admirer.

"Come on Ari, it's obvious," Hanna sits up from the LoveSac. "He even quoted something from yesterday's card."

"Guys, it can be anyone and that could be a coincidence." I roll my eyes, set my hot chocolate down on the coffee table.

"You just don't want to know who the person is," Kate mumbles.

"I don't see the point," I shrug my shoulders.

"The point is that the person obviously likes you and just wants you to be happy which is why they're doing this. A guy wouldn't do all this if they didn't give a crap about you." Hanna states. "Now what does today's card say?"

I take the envelope laying on the table next to me, opening it up to reveal an adorable penguin wearing a beanie on a snowy hill on the cover. I open the card to read the all too familiar writing.

Dearest Arianna,

I saw that you and your friends enjoyed decorating your home. I also noticed that you're wearing the necklace I got you. It looks amazing on you, so I'm glad you like it. Since you got a tree yesterday, that means it's time to get the most important items that go under the Christmas tree. The Christmas gifts. So I hope you enjoy shopping for your mother and friends. Don't forget the stocking stuffers.

Yours Truly,
Christmas Angel

"Ari, you're blushing but also look annoyed," Kate jokes.

"What does it say?" Hanna gets up and takes the card from me. "Oh, this is going to be fun," She laughs.

"What is it?" Kate goes to stand next to Hanna. She starts laughing while reading over her shoulder.

"My mother still hasn't even said anything about the house looking like the north pole," I tell them while waving my hands around the living room. "I should get started on my grave instead of buying her gifts."

"Girl, you're overreacting. There's no way she's going to kill you for this. Especially when you buy her gifts." Hanna sits next to me.

"Yeah, yeah, yeah," I get up from the couch. "Let's get this over with," Walking towards the front door.

Here we are walking around the mall, having no clue what to get for my wonderful mother. "I'll be right back, I have to go look for something," Hanna tells the two of us before walking into Victoria's Secret.

"Do you think she's getting two special items for her date with Samual?" Kate laughs softly beside me as we continue walking past the stores.

"There's no think to it, she's definitely getting something for their date." I laugh while nudging into her.

"Maybe you'll find something for your mom in here," Kate tells me while walking into Bath & Body Works.

I shrug my shoulders, following her into the store, the aroma of smelling goods flow through my nostrils. I place a shopping basket on my arm and start searching around. I notice Hanna's favorite fragrance, 'A Thousand Wishes,' and grab the large perfume bottle along with the lotion and place it into the basket. Walking over to where the candles are located, I see a couple that I believe that mom would enjoy. I pick them up smelling the beautiful aroma. Satisfied, I place them into the basket.

Now to find something that smells good that Kate might enjoy. I know she loves the holiday editions when they are out. I look around, noticing she's in the front of the store looking at the male products. Probably finding something for her dad or brother. I made my way over to the holiday section and there are these adorable holiday beauty bags with traveling size perfume and lotions inside. I take one that I believe she'll love and hurry to the cashier before Kate sees what I got. "That'll be $58," The cashier tells me. I slide my card into the machine while she places the items into a big bag. "Here you go."

"Thank you," I smile softly while taking the bag from her and start walking towards the entrance to wait for Kate. My phone goes off signaling that I got a text. Not surprised to see it was Hanna wondering where we are. I give her my destination, just to see her already walking this way. "Hey," I greet her.

"Guessing you found something for your mom?" She gestures towards my shopping bag.

"Yeah, but this is just the beginning. Still need to get her a few more things. How much did you get your mom?"

"I normally get my parents and brother 4 items each."

"So I need to get her 3 more items."

"There you are," I hear Kate walk up to us.

"Welcome back," I laugh. We begin walking towards another unknown location to continue shopping.

When we got done shopping, I went straight to Target to get wrapping paper and some boxes for some items. I was lucky that Hanna and Kate went into their cars so they couldn't see what I got them. The moment I started wrapping the gifts, I realized that I had to take the polaroid pictures myself. Which explains the crazy awkward pictures I am hanging up right now in my locker. Bet that'll give the mystery fella a good laugh.

"Now these are funny," I hear a familiar voice say from behind me.

"Shut up," I grumble while grabbing my books out of my locker before shutting it.

"Just stating the obvious," Colby tells me while walking beside me.

"What are you doing?" I question him.

"Walking to class," He states like it was extremely obvious. I stop walking when we reach my first class of the day. When I walk in, I sit down in my assigned seat.

"Are you following me?" I raise a brow at Colby when I look over to see him sitting down at a table.

He chuckles while shaking his head, "Did you hit your head, or are you seriously just realizing that we both have the same homeroom?" I don't say anything, just mouth 'oh' and avert my attention to my things. Pull my notebook out and hang my purse on my chair. I remove my hair from behind my ear to hide my face from him. Even though there was no topic on the board for us to write about, I just wrote random things on a blank sheet so my eyes were focused on something and not on Colby who I knew kept looking over at me.

"How could you not notice that Colby is in your homeroom?" Kate asks me.

"I don't know!" I say for what felt like the millionth time. "Guess the lack of sleep affected my memory." I shrug my shoulder while taking a bite of my salad.

"I'm definitely highlighting Colby's name on the list because I one hundred percent believe that it's him," Hanna states while taking the top off her green highlighter.

"It's not him!" I argue.

"Oh my gosh, Arianna wake up and smell the coffee because all the leads point towards him." Kate shoots and pushes the notebook towards me that has guys' names and any sort of hints that lead towards the admirer, which in fact shows that Colby has the most under his name.

I slide the list back towards them, not commenting about the subject, and just grab the velvet envelope out of my bag. I open it up and see a beautiful card that has a church on it surrounded by snow with a family dressed in vintage clothing walking towards it. I open the card to read the red ink.

My *Arianna,*

I hope you enjoyed the craziness of Christmas shopping. It's stressful, don't worry I got you something for Christmas but you'll have to wait till we meet to receive it. Now for today's task is going to be extremely fun. You're going to enjoy it, trust me. You and your wonderful friends are going to go sledding down a big snowy hill. Something I grew to love as a kid. So I know you'll love it as well.

Yours Truly,
Christmas Angel

"Please tell me one of you owns a sled," I look up at the two.

"I do, why?" Hanna questions. I pass her the card so she can read what the mystery person has assigned us for today. "Ooo, this is going to be fun! We can do this in my backyard since we have a big hill. My brothers and I always ride down it, and have a contest about who will make it down the hill first."

"Will your brothers let us use their sleds?" I ask.

"Heck, they'll probably join us."

"Oh, this will be fun," I tell her.

Bundled up, we're standing on top of the hill in Hanna's backyard with snow falling around us watching Hanna, her brothers, and Kate riding down it, snow flying up and probably hitting their faces. Laughing while Hanna's brother Robbie falls off his sled rolling down the rest of the hill before landing on his back softly laughing to himself.

"Okay," He stands up, dusting some of the snow off. "Ari, it's your turn," He smiles and points at me.

"Oh, no," I back away towards the white painted fence, while he picks his sled up and runs up the hill to me.

"Come on Arianna, you have to!" Kate cups her hands around her hand as she shouts from the bottom of the hill.

Robbie lays the sled on the edge of the hill, sits down on it with his legs crossed. "Sit," He pats behind him. Robbie is a year older than me, home from college. So it didn't feel weird sitting behind him, wrapping my arms around him to hold on for dear life. My hands clench tight together, eyes squeezed shut, biting the inside of my lip waiting for the possibility of falling off just like he did minutes ago. Robbie scoots us forward and soon we're flying down the hill, feeling the snow flow up and hit my face.

"You had your eyes closed the whole time," Hanna points out when we reach the bottom.

"At least I did it," I argued while getting up. Robbie takes a hold of my hand, gently pulling back towards the hill. "What are you doing?" I raise a brow at him.

"We're going to go do it right," He tells me.

"What?" I look at him before looking towards Hanna. She smirks and shrugs her shoulders, watching Robbie drag me back up the hill, pulling out my camera to prepare for comical moments to take.

"You're sitting in the front this time," He instructs.

"Oh, no I'm not," I protest.

"I'll hold the sled so you don't slide down without me," He holds the back of the sled, waiting for me to take a seat. I let out a breath and cautiously sat down, crossing my legs and taking hold of the thick string. A weight fills space behind me, signaling Robbie is taking his position, his legs lay beside me. "Keep your eyes open this time," He whispers before pushing the sled down the hill.

A smile breaks onto my face, watching the snow fly around us, everyone at the bottom cheering while we swish side to side making our way to them. It's a totally different experience from having my eyes closed. This time I understand why sledding is so much fun, the rush is amazing and the cold doesn't affect you.

"Want to do it again?" He asks.

"Definitely," I smile at him.

December 11th

Sledding was indeed fun but after a while, I felt like I was turning into a frozen popsicle. Hanna ended up lending me a pair of sweatpants and a sweater since my clothes were soaking wet. Her mother also made us some hot chocolate to drink while warming up in front of the fireplace.

"Arianna, right?" A boy questions in front of me, while I'm doing the Algebra 2 problem that's written on the board. It's basically how my English teacher gives us a morning prompt but instead, my Algebra 2 teacher gives us problems that make us want to jump off a cliff.

"Um, yeah," I awkwardly replied. "Why are you asking?"

He pulls out a red envelope and hands it out to me. "Someone wanted me to give this to you," he tells me before walking to take his seat.

"Wait," I turn to look over at him. "Who was it?"

"Sorry, I promised not to reveal the source," He

smirks, making me believe that he's friends with the mystery fella.

I sigh and slouch in my seat, pick up the envelope, and tear it open sliding out the card with two gingerbread people on the cover.

Dear Arianna,

I hope you enjoyed sledding, it's one of my favorite holiday activities. The rush going down the snowy hill is exhilarating. Now today, I'm craving something sweet which is making me think that you should build a gingerbread house. I have a feeling you never had the fun of creating one. Just a warning that it can be a little messy.

Yours Truly,
Christmas Angel

Sadly, today Kate and Hanna had plans after school so creating the gingerbread house is going to be just for my fun or torture. One of the two. I pulled into the driveway after stopping by Target to get a gingerbread kit and while getting out of my car, my eyes caught my mother's car inside the garage. This will be the first time in days I believe that we might see each other. I lock my jeep and start walking through the snowy path towards the front door.

A delicious aroma flows into my nose making

my taste buds dance. I remove my wet boots by the front door, set my backpack, and purse on the stairs before going into the kitchen with the Target bag. "This is surprising," I comment when my eyes see my mother cooking.

She turns to face me while smiling, "Is it a crime to cook my only child dinner on my day off?" She wipes her hands with a dish towel. "Now, what's surprising is that you decorated the house with Christmas decorations and put up a tree."

I swallow the invisible lump in my throat. "You're not mad are you?" I sat down at the island counter bar.

"Why would I be upset about all this?" She gestures to the decorations in the kitchen.

"Well, we never decorate for the holidays," I grab an apple out of the decorated bowl in front of me and start twisting the stem. "So I figured you'd dig me a grave for randomly putting up these decorations."

She laughs softly to herself. "I don't hate Christmas if that's what you think," she tells me while stirring whatever is in the small pot.

"Then why have we never celebrated it? You don't even buy gifts."

She signs softly, turning off the stove. "I'm sorry for that," She faces me again and leans on the island in front of me. "There's no excuse for me not celebrating the holidays with you. It's hard, I'm a single mom. I have to make sure to pay the bills and make sure there's food in the fridge for us to eat. I'm not superwoman."

I always thought my mother hated the holidays.

I never thought she didn't celebrate them because she was making sure that we don't end up on the streets. A soft smile appears on my face as I make my way to her. I wrap my arms around her, "I love you mom, thank you." I told her while I was hugging her tightly.

"Now, what do you have there?" She refers to the bag on the counter, wiping her eyes when I release her from the hug.

"Oh, I stopped by Target to get a gingerbread house kit," I walk over to the bag and pull the box out.

"Ooo, that sounds like a fun thing we can do together," she smiles.

"Wait," I set the box down. "You want to build it with me?" My smile grows bigger.

"Yes," She chuckles. "I'll fix our plate of food while you get everything set up and we can eat while we attempt to build it." She tells me.

"Sounds like a plan," I commented while I began to open the kit.

"It's going to fall!" I covered my wall watching my mom attempt to attach the roof pieces.

"You're paranoid, it's not going to fall," She assures me.

"Oh my god, mom. Yes, it is," I anxiously watch the bottom pieces shake. She removes her hands and not soon after the house fumbles down onto the cutting board we were building it on. "I told you so," I crossed my arms on my chest.

"I told you so," She mocks. "Let's try this again." She moves the pieces off the board and onto a plate. "Give me the icing," holding her hand out. I grab the icing tube, handing it to her while I reach for my camera. Softly laughing while I take a picture of her.

I don't remember the last time my mother and I spent time with each other like this so I want pictures to remember this moment. I'm actually thankful that my Christmas angel has put me through these tasks because I don't think this moment would have ever happened. My mother wouldn't have opened up to me about why we never celebrated the holidays. I would have always thought she despised them.

"Are you going to keep taking pictures or are you going to help me?"

"If I remember correctly, you made me stop helping because I kept eating the icing and candy." I set the camera down after taking a picture of me and my mother in the background holding two of the bottom pieces. "What do you want to help with?" I ask.

"Hold these together so I can work on the third wall," She instructs me.

"Yes, ma'am." She playfully smacks my head.

"Hey! What was that for?"

"Just a reminder to not eat the icing," She smiles.

Spending time with my mother, creating the most disastrous gingerbread house was something I needed. We normally just sit around the table or the counter bar and talk about each other's day but that was so rare because of her scheduling. I wish that we could have more of these moments together but I understand why mom works as hard as she does. I am happy that she plans to try her best to get Christmas off or get a day off that week, so we can have an actual Christmas. My mother even told me that she's going to go out shopping for gifts whenever she gets a chance.

"Hey," I smile at my two best friends who are walking towards me.

"Someone is in a good mood," Hanna jokes as she leans against the locker that's beside me.

"There's no way this could be from building a gingerbread house by yourself." Kate states.

"I didn't build it by myself," I tell both of them

while pulling the polaroids out of my purse.

"Who helped you? Was it a boy? Wait! Was it Colby?" Kate gets excited.

"Sorry, to disappoint you but my mother was the one who helped me," I laugh while hanging the pictures on my locker door before putting what I don't need inside it and grabbing my books.

"I thought she hated the holidays?" Hanna asked in a confused tone.

"I thought so as well but it turns out she loves the holidays," I say to them. As we walked down the school's hallway, I told them everything that happened yesterday night. We laugh about how much it was a disaster, even showed them a picture of the creation which makes us laugh even harder.

"Ms. Rose," The sound of my homeroom teacher calls out for me when I walk past the classroom.

"I'll see guys later," I tell Kate and Hanna before walking over to Mr. Anderson, yup that's right. My English teacher is also my homeroom teacher. Gotta love that. "I was seriously about to turn around before the tardy bell rang," I say while walking up to him.

"You're not in trouble," He chuckles. "Just wanted to hand this to you before I forget," He reaches out the familiar red envelope for me to take.

"Wait, who gave this to you?" I question.

"Sorry, not allowed to tell." He assures me, right when the bell rings. "Now, go take your seat."

I take the card out of the front pocket of my backpack while sitting down at my favorite table in the library. So far, I know that two people know who my secret admirer is and now it's slowly getting to me. There are 13 days until Christmas. I was never interested in finding out who he could be, but now for some reason, I truly want to know.

Smiling softly, I open the envelope to see a red nutcracker on the cover of the card. Today's adventure, reads:

Dearest Arianna,

Bet you're on the edge of your seat now to figure out who I am. Don't worry, the face behind these red ink words will be revealed to you soon. Until then enjoy having my cards delivered by my favorite trustworthy people;). That doesn't mean I'll no longer be checking the evidence of photos because I will be. Especially since I have random wrapped gifts to give you. That's a hint for the gift that will be inside your locker after the final bell rings. Now today's task is gonna be one for the books. It's getting your picture with Santa day!! Remember to let him know what you want for Christmas, so he makes sure it's delivered to you on Christmas!

Yours Truly,
Christmas Angel

"You have got to be kidding me," I say to myself. "What?" Kate questions as she magically appears in front of me. I slide the card to her, my eyes watch her fight back the laughter that wants to be set free as she reads what the secret admirer wrote. "I'm so going with you because I would love to see you visit Mr. Santa Claus." She slides the card back over to me and covers her mouth with her sleeve covered hand.

"I'm 17 years old, what 17-year-old goes to sit on Santa's lap?" I groan, leaning back propping my feet up on the wooden chair I'm sitting on.

"Um, a 17 year who still believes in Santa," Kate shrugs her shoulders and lets out a small laugh.

I wave my hands around, "Yeah, this 17-year-old doesn't." Kate just laughs even harder. "Oh, shut up," I grumble. "Where's Hanna?"

"You just told me to shut up which means I can't tell you," She smiles brightly at me.

I roll my eyes. "Why am I friends with you?"

"Because you don't want to die alone," She casually answers while she takes my chips out of my purse to snack on.

"I won't die alone because I have Hanna," I fire back and snatch my chips away from her.

Kate looks around and looks under the table, "I don't see her spending time with you during your lunch period," She jokes.

"Whatever," I roll my eyes and toss a chip into my mouth.

Here I am, standing around the food court in the mall waiting for Kate to return to my side. Hanna couldn't tag along because today she's finally going on her date with Samuel. Hanna explained to me that their sub made her stay in class, which is why she didn't get to spend my lunch with me. She also complained about how it wasn't fair that Kate was able to leave. Which I do agree, it doesn't make sense.

"I'm back!" Kate announces walking towards me with a cookie in one hand and a Starbucks drink in the other.

"You said you had to go to the bathroom!"

"I did, but then I saw Starbucks and it called out to me," She smiles sheepishly.

"Where is my drink?"

"Um," She looks down at hers. "Cookie?" She holds her cookie out towards me.

"Just take me to Santa already, so I can get this task over with." I start walking away from the entrance we came in from.

"Do you think you're going to get anything from mystery boy over the weekend?" Kate questions while munching on the chocolate chip cookie in her hand.

"I don't know, maybe. He did drop off a few items last weekend."

We walk towards the center of the mall, where we see the big north pole display. The line to Santa wasn't long, which I'm thankful for because that means I can get this picture done and over with fast. "Maybe he's here right now," Kate stands on her tiptoes observing the people around us.

"Maybe," I look around as well. "But what's the point in looking when we have no clue who the mystery boy is. Only two people know." I tell her while we join the line to Santa.

"Wait?" Kate looks at me. "Who knows?"

"Well, Mr. Anderson, and apparently a guy in my Algebra 2 is mystery boy's friend." I cross my arms over my chest, taking a small step forward when the line moves a couple of steps.

"Didn't you ask both of them, who he is?"

"No Kate, I decided to go to Narnia instead. Of course, I questioned them but obviously, they wouldn't give me a single detail."

"Okay, okay." She takes a sip of coffee. "Is that Derek?" She whispers while trying to not burst into laughter as we walk closer, pointing towards a guy dressed all up as an Elf.

My eyes examine the fella standing where the line begins. Green tights, fake pointy ears, funny look-ing shoes, still can't get a clear view of his face but some pieces of his black hair sticking out of the green and red hat he's wearing. His attention stays on the little kids until they're sitting on Santa. Then, he finally looks over at Kate and me.

"Aren't you two a little too old for Santa?" He points at us while raising a brow.

"Um," I pause trying to think of a response.

"Aren't you a little tall to be an elf?" Kate shoots back.

"Did you forget about Buddy the Elf?" He cross-es his arms.

"That was a movie," She copies his action.

"Based on a tall Elf."

I covered my mouth, watching the two bicker over something so stupid. If it wasn't for mister Santa shouting for Derek the Elf to send along the next kid, I honestly believe they would go on for hours.

"Wait, what's your number?" Derek asks Kate.

She looks over at me and mouths 'Hold on', before exchanging phones with him and he whispers something causing her to walk back over with a smile.

"Sooo," I wiggle my brows at her.

"Well, he's definitely not your mystery boy," She links her arm with mine as we walk up to Santa.

"I put money on the kitchen counter, so you can order yourself food when you get hungry," My mother kisses my cheek before walking to the front door.

"Okay, thank you," I smiled softly at her.

"I don't get off until tomorrow morning but I'm gonna stop by the store on my way home."

"So you'll probably be home before noon and go straight to bed?"

"Yeah, sounds about right."

"Okay, have fun at work, love you."

"Have fun with your binge-fest, love you too." With that, she walks out the door.

I pushed the blanket off me, got off the couch, and made my way towards the kitchen. I open up random cabinets until I finally find my Fritos that I hid so Kate or Hanna couldn't steal them. I prop myself on the counter, grab my phone out of my hoodie pocket to send a text in our group chat asking if either of them wants to come over and I'll order us pizza.

Not bothering on waiting for a response, I opened the Dominos app to place an order on one meat lover and one supreme pizza, along with a 2 liter coca cola and brownies. I go back into the living room and wait for Kate and Hanna to turn up.

Most teenagers, I feel, would be partying right now but here I am, cuddling under a blanket munching on my chips, and scrolling through Netflix trying not to rewatch Grey's Anatomy for the hundredth time, which is why I'm going to rewatch The Vampire Diaries instead. Such a holly jolly show to binge watch during this lovely snowy holiday season.

I groan when the sound of the doorbell fills the house, "when in the world did you guys decide to now be polite and not just waltz right in?" I grumble while walking to open the door. "And you guys are not Kate and Hanna nor the pizza guy," I state when a large group is revealed after I open the door.

They all smile big and start randomly singing Silent Night. Instead of being a scrooge and shutting the door on them, I lean against the door frame and listen to them. We never had Christmas Carolers come to our house so this was a big surprise for me. They sang amazingly together, so soothing, and not one person was off-key. After they finished Silent Night, they began singing Hallelujah. I don't know the original artist but

Kate constantly played the version that Pentatonix did. The carolers reminded me of that version.

It was so beautiful that it made my eyes tear up. While wiping the tears away, a red envelope catches my eye that's sticking out of someone's bag. There's no way that it's the envelope I think it is. I bite the inside of my lip, trying not to stare at it and focus on the carolers.

They sang two more songs before walking away. I clapped my hands together and told them that their performance was incredible. "This is for you," a lady tells me while handing me the envelope. It's a little heavier than normal and bulky.

"Thank you," I say in an almost whisper. "Wait!" I called out as she began walking to catch up with the others. "Who gave this to you?"

"Sorry, I'm not allowed to say," she smiles at me before joining the carolers.

"Of course not," I mutter as I enter the house, walking over to reunite with the comfy warm couch. Sliding my finger to open the envelope, I pull the heavy bulky card out. It has a picture of Christmas carolers singing in the snow on the cover. I shake my head and open it to read it but my eyes widen to see a charm bracelet taped on the unwritten side.

I pull it off and remove the tape before admiring each charm hanging off of it. A snowflake, a mug that resembles hot chocolate, an ice skate, an envelope that says "my love", a Christmas tree, a sled, a gingerbread house, Santa, and lastly two Christmas carolers. I smile softly while examining each one, connecting the secret dots that tell me they all resemble each task my admirer has given me so far. I clasp the bracelet around my wrist before finally reading the red ink that's inside the card.

My Arianna,

Hope you loved the surprise I sent to your home. It's not Christmas without the wonderful Carolers singing at your doorsteps. I happily asked them to sing my favorite Christmas songs. I'm gonna make sure to ask you which one was your favorite when you finally get to meet who is behind these cards. I also hope you love the charm bracelet my mother helped me put together.

Yours Truly
Christmas Angel

December
14th

Sunlight beams against my face causing a groan to leave my lips. I rub my eyes preparing to open them. Kate is laying in front of me on the couch as we laid feet to face sharing a blanket. I slowly remove myself off the couch, careful not to wake her. I stretch out my back while taking notice that Hanna was still curled up on the Love-Sac where she passed out last night. The tv was still on, showing the menu screen of the last movie we watched from our movie marathon.

The coffee table was covered in our snack volcano. An empty bowl with just popcorn kernels, two pizza boxes, one with a single slice left and another full of pizza crusts. Soda cans were all over, some smashed and the others probably half empty. I make my way to the kitchen to grab the trash can, and begin cleaning up the living room before my mom comes home.

"Hello sleeping beauty," I greet Hanna who slowly enters the kitchen as I wash the bowl that had the popcorn in it.

"Coffee," She groans, grabbing one of the clean mugs off the strainer before pouring herself the fresh coffee I made just in case my mom wanted a cup. She moans softly while taking a sip. "Now, that hit the spot."

I laugh softly, "Guessing Kate is still asleep?"

"Yeah," She answers while sitting at the counter. "Is there anything I can help with?"

"All that needs to be done is the pizza boxes. They need to be thrown out and the trash bag." I nod my head where they were located.

"Arianna, can you explain why there were flowers on our porch?" My mom questions while entering the house.

"What?" I tossed the dish towel onto the counter, following Hanna to the front door where my mother was standing, bags hanging from her arms while her hands held red vibrant Poinsettias that had a red velvet envelope with my name written on it. A soft smile spreads across my face as I take the flowers from my mom before returning back into the kitchen.

I set the flowers on the counter and removed the envelope to read the card that was inside. The cover was a truck covered in snow with trees in its trunk. For some reason it made me laugh while opening it up to read the words my Christmas angel has written.

Dearest *Arianna,*

I hope you enjoy these vibrant red Poinsettias, which are known to be the Christmas flowers. My father and I went out this morning to get them for my mom as a surprise. So, I randomly decided why not surprise the most beautiful girl in school that I'm slowly getting to fall in love with this amazing holiday season. Hope you love them.

> *Yours Truly,*
> *Christmas Angel*

"I never received flowers before," I say in almost a whisper, placing the card back inside the envelope. Keeping my eyes on the beautiful flowers set in front of me.

December 15th

"Okay, everyone settle down," my homeroom teacher demands. We all got situated in our seats, waiting for him to continue. "It's the last week of school, before winter break. Which means it's Giving Week." He picks up a clipboard off his desk. "Now, last week I had you guys sign up for stations that you'll be doing all week during your free period." Mr. Anderson examines the list while walking to stand in front of us. "Each of your last periods has been turned into your free periods, if your station is off school grounds, you'll make your way to the front of the school to wait for your chaperones who will supervise you. They'll make sure you'll be back in time so you don't miss your bus." He explains. "Any questions?" His eyes run over us looking for a hand to call upon.

"If we have our own car, can we drive it to our location?" Justin asked when Anderson called on him.

Anderson looks over a piece of paper, that must

be the rule sheet the principal sent out. "Yes, but you must be there when everyone arrives, and if you don't show up, automatic detention."

Justin nods his head, while some students cheer and grumble. Some are probably complaining since they can't get away with ditching the rest of the day. Lucky me, every year I always get to hang out with the art teacher and mess with the clay while everyone does Christmas activities.

I doodle on my notebook as Mr. Anderson begins calling out people's names on what they'll be doing this week. "Arianna Rose." My head shot up so fast that I pulled a muscle in my neck.

"Mr. Anderson, there has to be a mistake. I didn't sign up for anything." I explain while holding my hand up.

He doesn't say anything, just walks up to my desk and places a red envelope on my desk before going back to the front of the room. "Oh, of course," I whisper to myself as I grab the envelope to open it.

My Arianna,

You're probably wondering why on earth would I sign you up for fun activities for our school's giving week. Well, I knew you weren't going to sign yourself up since you love spending giving week in the art room. And Christmas time, a holiday dedicated to giving back. You can hate me but I know you truly don't ;)

Yours Truly
Christmas Angel

I grumble to myself as I put the glitter wreath covered card back inside the velvet envelope. "Where am I going?" I ask Mr. Anderson, annoyed because he knows who the mystery fella is.

"You're gonna be helping out at an Elementary school." He smirks before going back to naming who's in what group.

I let out a deep sigh, climbing down the small bus stairs. "Okay, there's twelve of you and I'm going to partner you all up before sending you to the classroom you're going to be working with today. Each day this week, you'll be helping out with the class you're assigned. The teachers already know who they're suspecting, and I'll do random check-ins to make sure no one is skipping. Remember that if you don't show up or not where you're supposed to, you'll spend the rest of the week in deten-tion." Mrs. Steele tells the group.

"Now, when I call your names please go to your partner until I give you the teacher and room number you'll be going to." She flips a page on her clipboard and begins naming each pair, one by one, students start walking to their partner. Some were happy they got their best friend and others were annoyed. "Arianna and Justin," I stay put, not wanting to move. In the corner of my eye I see Justin with a smug look walking towards me.

"Hey," He greets me.

"Hi," I softly respond.

"How was the cookie dough bites?"

My eyes widen, shocked that he remembers giving me the last box ten days ago from our encounter. The only reason I remember that was because Kate and Hanna were keeping track of who I bump into, just to narrow down who the admirer could be. "Um, they were good."

"They better have been, I had to go the whole night without them."

"You're the one who gave them away, I would have never been that generous." I smiled.

Justin lets out a soft chuckle, "I'll remember that the next beautiful girl gets heartbroken when I take the final box of cookie dough bites." He teases.

I roll my eyes at his comment, before I could say something Mrs. Steele begins assigning students their destination.

"Arianna and Justin, you two will be working with Ms. Robbins' class whose room is 156." She hands us a piece of paper, which happens to be the school's map with a red sharpie circling the room.

"Okay, so I already split the class up into two groups. The small group you'll be in charge with." Ms.Robbins explains to us. "One group is going to do fun creative Christmas decor, the other is waiting on our reading carpet prepared to be read to." She continues. "Justin, you can work with the kids in the craft section, and Arianna, you will read to the others." She opens the classroom's room, revealing the little ones in their areas, talking among themselves.

I make my way over to the carpet, smiling softly as I take a seat on the miniature that's facing the kids. "Hi," I say sweetly. "I'm Arianna, and we're gonna be spending a lot of time together this week. So what book do you guys want me to read to you?" I turn to look at the bookshelf next to us, scanning over the collection of child stories the teacher has.

"Read your favorite Christmas story!" One of the little ones shouts.

"I actually don't have a favorite, how about one of you pick out your favorite and I'll read it." A little boy gets off the carpet, makes his way over to the bookcase to grab a book to hand over to me. I smile softly, look down at the red hardcover book, with a black sketch of a cartoon character. "How The Grinch Stole Christmas," I read out the title.

I look over at them as I'm reading, feeling all warm at how they're so intrigued with the story. Some saying the lines with me. It's funny but extremely adorable. I continue reading and showing them the illustrations, laughing as they laugh. Right till the very last page, where they beg for me to read another book.

December 16th

"Ms. Arianna, look what I made," One of the kids with a cheerful smile calls out to me. I walk over to her to examine the creation she made. My group is doing Christmas crafts today. Justin is busy reading stories to his group and I've been taking turns helping each kid while attempting to make snowman and snowwoman on construction paper while using glitter.

"That's so cute!" I gush over the little girl's reindeer made out of brown construction paper, a pink polka-dot bow, and a bright red nose.

"It's Rudolph's sister!" She smiled big at me.

"I love it!"

Her sky blue eyes glimmered with excitement. She looked down at her creation and grabbed a crayon to write something on it. "Here!" She hands me the paper, I look over at what she just did. My eyes start to tear up, To Ariana, From Macy.

I bent down to her, "Thank you," giving her a

side hug. "I'm gonna hang this up in my room."

"Really?" Her eyes lit up.

"Yes, I'll take a picture when I do so and show you the proof tomorrow."

"Pinky promise?" She sticks her pinky out.

I wrap mine with hers, "Pinky promise."

"Arianna, can you come here please?" Ms. Robbins asks me.

"I'll be right back, create something new," I tell Macy before walking over to Robbins' desk. "Yes?"

"This is for you," She hands me a red envelope.

"Thank you," I say before taking a seat at an empty table to read what Mr. Mystery Man has written for me today. Carefully ripping open the envelope, to slide the snow globe glitter card and read his semi messy red ink writing.

Dearest Arianna,

My family has this tradition where we pick one special family to leave gifts for on their porch anonymously. It started when I was in Kindergarten. I talked to Ms. Robbins, and she helped me pick a student you will shop for and deliver gifts to. On a small folded paper inside the envelope with the child's name, the amount of family members that live in the house and their age. Along with the address. Do not reveal who you are, just who each gift is to. Enjoy:)

Yours Truly,
Christmas Angel

I put my car in park after getting back to school and decided that I'll do my shopping spree and complete today's task before heading home. Of course, I asked Hanna and Kate to help me out, being the amazing friends they are, they agreed to meet me here at Target. Grabbing my purse and exiting the vehicle, I begin making my way towards Target's entrance while scrolling on my phone to review the family Mystery man and Ms. Robbins had picked for me.

The family I received is a little boy who's 5 years old and has an older sister about 14. The mother is a baker at a supermarket and the dad works overnights at a store. So my shopping won't be extravagant, but I'm thinking of 3 items for the kids and 2 or 3 items for each parent. No clue on what to get everyone but I know boys love playing with cars, so at least I have a little idea.

"So, where are you starting?" Hanna claps her hands together when I meet up with them inside.

"Well, we can start with the little boy and afterwards find things for his sister," I suggest.

"Sounds like a good plan," Kate tells us while grabbing a shopping cart.

We decided to get the little boy a Hot Wheels race track with a couple of Hot Wheels Cars. For his sister, we decided to get her a few make-up items and a journal. The father was hard to figure out, none of us knew what to get him. We figured just to get him a wallet, a mug with some cookies. We also agreed to get the mother a book, bath bombs, and chocolates.

After our shopping spree, we went straight to my house to wrap the items. Labeling which items belong to who. Now we're sitting in my vehicle, outside the house, patiently waiting for someone to open the front door. So we can take a polaroid picture proving that we did indeed complete the task. I shush Kate and Hanna when the front door slowly opens, revealing a familiar little boy.

The little boy who insisted on me to read his favorite Christmas story whose eyes are brown and has short black hair with the most charming smile that can make anyone smile. I watch him closely as he examines the gifts, getting excited when he sees the ones labeled with his name. He runs inside, and seconds later back on the front porch with his parents and sister. The mom and dad scan the area causing Hanna, Kate, and me to squat down in the vehicle afraid they'll come to us if we got spotted. The sister grabbed her gifts and helped her brother with his before walking into the house. The parents looked around one last time before grabbing theirs and following the kids inside.

"That was seriously the most heartwarming thing I ever witnessed," Hanna breathes out.

"Same," I softly respond still looking at the front door.

December 17th

Tomorrow is the Elementary School Christmas Concert, so I'm currently sitting in the gym while Ms. Robbins' class is rehearsing. There's nothing for me to do, which is why I'm working on homework that a random teacher decided to give out even though it's the end of the semester.

"Why are you sitting here doing homework?" Justin questions, standing in front of me.

"Maybe because there's nothing for us to do."

"Now that's a lie."

I raise my head, "No, it's the truth. The kids are practicing for their show tomorrow. Ms. Robbins' told us that we can do whatever."

"No, no." He takes my notebook off my lap, "She said we can either help with the costumes and set or we can sit around to catch up on assignments from any of our classes." He tells me while placing my notebook in my bag.

I roll my eyes, letting out a breath, "I have no skill in sewing. How do you suspect me of helping out in the costume department," crossing my arms over my chest.

Justin shakes his head, smiling like I just made a joke. "Robbins already cut out the cardboard the kids will be wearing as costumes. We just have to paint them, and string them together." He holds his hand out for me to take. Groaning as I take it causing Justin to laugh while pulling me up off the ground. "Man, you act like it's going to kill you."

"Maybe it will, who knows," I shrug. "Make sure to have whoever is making my tombstone engrave, 'Cause of death: being forced to make child Christmas costumes instead of doing my homework,'" I say in a sarcastic tone.

"Oh boohoo, that homework isn't even going to count for the end of the semester grades." He mocks while walking towards the cut out cardboard pieces. I mock his words under my breath with my arms folded over my chest, slowly following behind him. Justin stops suddenly, causing me to run into his hardback, he holds a red envelope above his shoulder. "I heard that," He tells me in a smug tone. "And this is for you."

He doesn't move, just stands there with his back that felt like a brick wall towards me. I stand on my tiptoes, reaching up to take a hold of the velvet envelope between my fingers, bringing my lower lip between my lips anxiously intrigued to know what the mystery writer wrote for me today. "Wait!" I look up at him, my tone makes him stop walking and turn towards me, revealing his mischievous smile. His eyes scream as if he knew what words are going to leave my lips. "You know?"

"Know what?" He holds back a laugh.

"You know exactly what I'm talking about!"

"Do I?" He acts clueless, making his voice go high before turning on his heels to walk towards the craft section.

"Justin!" I grab his arm, feeling his hard biceps.

He shakes his head, amused by how irritated I had become. "Arianna, what can I help you with? Do you not know how to decorate a cardboard cutout of a Christmas tree?"

I slap his chest, "Cut the crap, who's been writing these cards to me?" I demand.

Justin holds his hands up like he's surrendering to be arrested. "Sorry, but I swore not to speak his name."

"This isn't Harry Potter! He's not Lord Voldermort! Who is he?!" Growing frustrated.

"I seriously can't tell you, I'm sorry," His tone goes soft. He turns back around, grabs random colors of paint and brushes and picks a cardboard cut-out, and begins painting. I stay put and open the envelope, pulling out a simple decorate card with the word 'Peace' printed on the front.

Dear Arianna,

The feeling of seeing a family get emotional over the items my family and I leave for them, makes my heart feel like it's about to be burst out of my chest. I really hope the

"You gotta be joking," I whisper.

"Stop laughing," I grumble, hiding my face with my hands. Currently sitting at the mall, where little kids write out their Christmas letters and place them in the metal red box that apparently the mailman or woman comes to mail them to Santa. Kate and Hanna are of course sitting across from me, watching me get annoyed at them laughing about how the admirer is making me do the most ridiculous thing ever. Well, tie it with taking a picture with Santa for being the most ridiculous thing.

"Sorry, sorry," Hanna tries to calm herself, "It's just that I haven't written a letter to Mr. Clause since I was in the 3rd grade." She bites down on her lower lip to contain her laughter.

Kate stuffs her mouth with her Dippin Dots while struggling not to laugh. Pretty sure she looks like she's going to choke. Can you choke on ice cream?

I look down at the blank sheet of paper, trying to figure out what to write. I'm not a little girl, I don't want a plastic barbie doll, dollhouse, a dog that walks on its own. I nibble on my lower lip, doodling on the corner of the paper, waiting for inspiration. Just something to write.

"What the heck do I write?!" I toss my pencil across the table, frustrated about this stupid idea.

"Write that you want him to get you a boyfriend?" Hanna jokes.

"Or a lifetime of cookie dough bites," Kate pitches in.

Hanna nudges her, "That's a smart idea, do that!" She hands back my pencil and points toward the paper. I shake my head, laughing as I begin writing.

Dear Santa,

I honestly think this is extremely cheesy. I'm a High School student, working on graduating, trying to keep my grades above an F. I know there's no such thing as Santa, so basically I'm writing this letter to no one. The only reason I'm even doing this is that a mystery person keeps leaving me Christmas cards, assigning me tasks to complete without leaving a single clue of who they are. Today's task is to write to you, telling you what I would like for Christmas. Santa, I have no clue what I would like. Never ponder about it. My friends told me to ask for a boyfriend, and a lifetime of cookie dough bites. Both of those I wouldn't mind, and definitely won't complain if I see the items under my tree. Maybe, if you are real and everyone is lying that you don't exist, and you're able to make this come true, can you make sure to bring Christmas into my home every year. Just so my mother and I can cherish it, create traditions, bring happiness, and give me something to finally look forward to.

Love,
Arianna Rose

December 18th

Ever since I wrote my letter to Santa, I can't stop pondering on why people write those letters? If they ever receive what they wish for and where those letters go off to? Does the post office toss them out or does someone actually go out of their way to help those kids get the toy of their dreams? Most importantly, why did my admirer have me write one?

When I got to school, I did my daily task of hanging the polaroid evidence of writing my letter and mailing it off. Now I'm in my natural habitat when lunch time hits for me. When I went to my locker, no card was there to give me my next holiday task. Makes me slightly sad and curious on when it'll magically appear. I wonder what's going to happen when Christmas break arrives, if this game will keep going.

I look at my polaroid camera, thinking about how I've been enjoying this experience. I'm starting to believe the admirer is Justin but I also believe he's too obvious that it's him. My pencil is tapping a way on the list I started creating with all the guys I bumped into since this game has start. I'm turning into my best friends.

"Hey, hey, hey."

Right on cue I hear Hanna's voice. I look up to see Hanna smiling as she sits across from me with Kate by her side.

"So does Chemistry not exist to you guys now?" I raise my brow at them.

"Give us a break, it's two days before Winter Break. Classes are basically over with." Hanna shrugs her shoulders before reaching over to take my chips again.

"Plus thanks to having a sub, we don't have work to do beside watching Christmas movies." Kate pipes in, her eyes looking at the notebook in front of me. "What do you have there?" She smiles at me before leaning closer.

"Nothing," I close it fast hoping she didn't get a good look.

"Yeah, right." Kate reaches her hand to snatch it. She flips through it until she finds the page. "Well, well, well, Hanna look what we have here."

Hanna leans over to look at the page, "Well looks like our dear Arianna is invested in this admirer than she has led on."

Their smiles grow as they examine the small list of names. "Justin, Derek, Colby, and Samual," Kate names off. "Why is there a star by Justin's name?"

I let out a groan and rub my hands over my face,

"That's who I believe is the admirer but I think it's too obvious to be him."

"Why do you think it's too obvious?" Hanna questions.

"Because he's the one I've seen the most and he's the one who handed me yesterday's card."

"That is true but you never know, sometimes the obvious one that stands out is the one," Kate tells me.

"Plus you won't know for sure until the 25th." Hanna winks before popping a Cheeto in her mouth.

Kate grabs my pen and starts scribbling over someone's name before handing my notebook over.

"Why is Derek's name eliminated?" I smirk at her.

"No reason," Kate smiles while leaning back.

The bell rings signaling it's time for us to head towards the next class that wants to destroy us. I gather my things and follow Kate and Hanna out of the library and make my way towards my locker just to see the red envelope tape onto my locker.

I smile as I open the velvet envelope to see the glittery card with a horse wearing a wreath on the cover. I open the card to finally read the handwriting of the mystery person.

My Arianna,

You probably thought it was silly to write a letter to Santa but it's one of the traditions in my family to make the holiday season magical. Today, you're going to attend the Christmas play at the Elementary school you've been volun-

teering at.

Yours Truly
Christmas Angel

Here I am standing in the Elementary school's gymnasium with Kate and Hanna by my side. Staking out from the far back to see if any of the guys on my list show up. We already took my picture showing that I was here as proof of completing the task. We have been here for what feels like hours watching families find seats to watch their kids perform cute skits.

Brings back memories from when I was their age. We did a skit for Rudolf the rednosed reindeer and we wore antlers and a red nose that lit up. It was so much fun, that was back when we did celebrate Christmas before my mom got busy with work. If I remember correctly, that was also the last school event my father attended. I was in kindergarten. A bittersweet memory.

"Do you see any of them?" I wish.

"No, it's too crowded and hard to tell who people are from the back of the head. Especially guys." Kate answers.

"Yeah, Kate, right. It also doesn't help since some of them are wearing hats." Hanna pipes in.

"Well, we should finally find a place to sit. The show will begin soon." I tell them.

Of course the quest to figure out my admirer won't be as easy as I hoped it would be.

December
19th

Friday, finally! The final day before winter break begins! An exciting day, everyone I walk past is all talking about their plans for the break. Meanwhile, mine is just sitting around the house or hanging out with Hanna and Kate, as well as counting down the days until my admirer shows his face.

6 days. 6 more days until I finally come face to face with the person who's been putting me on random Christmas tasks.

Last night it was fun watching the Christmas play. The kids did Frosty the Snowman, and Rudolf the rednosed reindeer, along with other classic Christmas songs. All grades did performances.

On our way out we did see all the guys on my list, super ironic. Luckily, Derek is no longer a suspect since he and Kate are dating. She finally admitted to them being an item.

I'm curious about how I'm going to be showing

my admirer that I completed my tasks over the break since I won't be able to place my pictures in my locker like I've been doing these past weeks.

As I get closer to my locker, I look cautiously around looking for a familiar face. Kate and Hanna were nowhere in sight, but one thing did catch my attention. Justin, Derek, and Colby hanging out by the water fountain with another guy that doesn't look so familiar to me.

"What are we staring at?" Hanna questions.

"Oh my gosh!" I jump at the sound of Hanna's voice causing her and Kate to laugh.

I look back over at the group of fellas to see if they heard me freak out, relief washes over me when they are still in their huddle chatting.

"Ah, now I see what we're staring at." Hanna nudges me.

"Yeah, do you guys know who that one guy is that's standing between Justin and Colby?"

"That's Nick, he's in my bio-lab class," Kate tells me.

"Do you think he's part of the secret admirer stuff?" I glance over at her.

Kate shrugs her shoulders, "I have no clue, but at this point, I wouldn't cut him out. He is a quiet dude, far as I know he isn't horrible."

I look over at the four guys one more time before walking with Kate and Hanna to our movie room destination.

We're currently sitting in our homeroom watching the classic holiday movie Home Alone, it's probably my favorite since it's not really circling around Christmas, just how the boy got left at home and is now saving the house from being robbed.

I feel a tap on my shoulder causing me to look behind me just to see a girl handing me the red envelope I've been waiting for.

"Who gave you this?" I whisper trying not to disturb anyone from the movie.

'Sorry.' She mouths before walking back to her seat.

I glance around to find the suspect but it's too dark and some have their heads down. I nudge Hanna to get her attention. She looks over at me raising her brow. I show her the envelope and nod toward the door.

Hanna taps Kate to get her in the loop and we all quietly walk toward the door to read the card.

"Okay, get to reading," Kate softly said.

I open the velvet envelope carefully to reveal the cute card with Christmas cookies scattered on it. After admiring the cover, I finally open the card to read the red ink.

My *Arianna,*

I hope you enjoyed the Christmas play, I saw you standing in the back with Kate and Hanna. I used to attend that school when I was little, it was fun going back and being

"He was there?!" Hanna nearly shouts causing Kate and me to shush her. "Sorry." She smiles.

"Of course, he was there, why am I not surprised." I press my back against the wall.

"I have an idea," Kate tells us. "What if we have all the guys we believe to be the suspect to join us in making the Christmas cookies?"

"That's not a bad idea," Hanna looks at me.

"Are you sure?" I look between the two.

"They all practically know about the whole thing, so it won't be creepy to make them get involved in the activity," Hanna explains.

"I'll text Derek telling him to have the guys be at your house right when school ends and be ready to make cookies." Kate pulls out her phone and begins texting.

Sounds like tonight is going to be festive.

"Colby, that is way too much icing!" I laugh while looking at his now bloody Santa.

"What are you talking about?" His dimples break
out as he smiles at me.

"It looks like your Santa got murdered." I try to
hold back more of my laughter.

He looks down at his cookie and starts to laugh,
"Well it's not done yet, I need to add his belt and cotton."

"Uh, huh." I smile, "Good luck with that." I pat
his shoulder and go to one of the cabinets where my
mom keeps the baking items to look and see if she has
any sprinkles. I want white ones for my snowflakes.

This has been a fun and extremely entertain-
ing evening. We attempted to make the cookie dough
from scratch, which ended up with flour being every-
where since Derek declared a flour battle with the guys.
Stain-dyed hands from making different color icings,
from Colby's murdered Santa we're going to need to
make more red icing. A lot of egg shells scattered from
our mini competition who can crack an egg perfectly
one-handed, which Kate happily won.

Now we're finally doing what the whole night is
intended for, decorating Christmas cookies. Along with
a competition who would make the best gingerbread
man/woman.

"Arianna, we need to take a picture for the admirer!" Hanna shouts over the music.

"Okay!" I jump down from the counter after
retrieving the white sprinkles my mom for some reason
had at the very top shelf. "Everyone gather around!" I
couldn't help but laugh at how ridiculous this picture is

going to be. All of us were covered in flour and decorative icing.

This night won't be forgotten.

December
20th

 Last night when the guys' left we kept an eye on the mailbox to see if one of them was going to open it. While they were helping clean up the kitchen, I went outside to place the envelope in the mailbox just like the admirer told me to do. Sadly, none of them did. They knew that's why we wanted them here.

What they didn't know is that I stood up last night waiting for them. There was no way they were going to wait until the sun was back in the sky. So when I saw him pull up on his bike, and reach to get the envelope, I waited till he left to go outside to see if he left one for me. I was disappointed when he didn't. More disappointed when I couldn't catch a glimpse of his face.

Now I'm sitting on the couch after inspecting the kitchen, seeing if we missed a spot that needs to be cleaned. Kate and Hanna left early this morning after mom made us breakfast.

"Mom, did you check the mail?"

"Yes, I went to get it while you were cleaning!" She yells from upstairs.

"Did I get anything?"

"In your room!"

I rush up the stairs as quickly as I can and storm into my room just to see a yellow envelope that looks like it could hold important documents. It's not the red velvet one that I'm waiting to receive. I look at the envelope, confused about the handwriting, it's identical to the one I've been reading all month.

I open the envelope just to find two items. A CD case and a red envelope. A smile breaks out on my face as I tear it open to read the card that has musical notes scattered to look like a Christmas tree on the cover.

Dearest Arianna,

I know what your plan was for yesterday, eager to find out who I am, are we? I bet you're disappointed that your plan wasn't successful. Sorry cupcake, but don't worry from the sound of the event it seemed fun making those cookies. That's right, I wasn't there. To cheer you up, I made you a CD filled with Christmas songs I enjoy and you do as well. 5 more days to go!

Yours Truly
Christmas Angel

Of course, he wasn't here. Why am I not surprised?! If he wasn't in my house, who would he be?! Justin, Nick, and Samuel didn't show up. It could be one of them.

"Agh!" I fall back onto my bed and grab one of my pillows to scream into.

After a few moments of pondering my life decisions away underneath my pillow, I rose from the regretful death and finally retrieved the CD from under the yellow envelope.

He drew his own album cover for it, making it all Christmassy. On the back has the list of songs he downloaded onto the disk.

Arianna's Christmas Playlist
Hope You Love It

Mistletoe by Justin Bieber
Silent Night by Pentatonix
Winter Wonderland/ Sleigh Ride by Dolly Parton
O Holy Night by Celine Dion
Jingle Bell Rock by Bobby Helms
Officially Christmas by Dan & Shay
Santa Baby by Gwen Stefani
White Christmas by Frank Sinatra

My face hurts from smiling so much, no one has ever made me a playlist, let alone go out of their way and burn it onto a cd for me. Whoever this person is, they got me hooked now.

I make my way to my closest and dig around on the upper shelf for my old cd player to set up to listen to the songs my admirers picked out for me. I lay on my bed, close my eyes, and smile as the music starts to play.

December
21st

My mom had to force me out of my room last night to eat because I didn't want to stop listening to the CD. She did help me take my picture proof, which she happily offered to place in the mailbox as she heads off to work this morning.

As I walk down the stairs, I take notice of the beautifully wrapped presents under the tree. I smile softly knowing my mom added to it. I'm thankful for this journey, it's bringing excitement to this holiday for us. I always try to stay up for when my mom comes home from work just so I can tell her about the task that I was sent on that day. If I'm unable to, I make sure to wake up early before she goes off to work.

My attention gets taken away by the sound of the doorbell. I rush to the door just to meet with no one but a rectangle-wrapped present with a gold ribbon. I glance around and see no one around, not even someone running away. I picked up the gift and walked into the kitchen. I lifted the bow to see if there was a tag addressing who it was to but there wasn't one.

I stare at the box, contemplating if I should open it or wait until my mother comes home tonight. Curiosity gets the best of me and I search through the drawers in the kitchen searching for the scissors. Once I find them, I go back to the present to cut the gold ribbon that is wrapped around the gift. I tear open the red wrapping paper and lift the lid to the box just to see a sweater and the red envelope I've been waiting for.

I slide the card out of the envelope, to see it has a funny Christmas sweater on the cover.

My Arianna,

I hope you love the CD I burnt for you, it took a long time to narrow it down to nine songs. Today's task is that you will be attending an ugly sweater party. I provided you with a sweater to wear, I hope I got the right size for you. Can't wait to see you there. The address is below.

Don't get lost!
Christmas Angel

Here I am standing outside the house that my admirer has sent me to. Of course, I dragged Kate and Hanna with me. According to them, this house belongs to Derek. Apparently, he is known to throw parties since he's on the basketball team so I'm not surprised my admirer has me attending a party that he's not even hosting. Doesn't help me at all.

When we enter the house, Kate ditches us to go find Derek leaving Hanna and I to scout out the party. Everyone is wearing creative Christmas sweaters, some looking like they made them themselves. The house is decked out in Christmas decorations and Christmas music is playing. People are dancing and laughing, and having an amazing time.

Hanna and I make our way through the house, trying to find the kitchen where all the goodies will be displayed. We worm our way through the crowd, trying not to bump into anyone.

"Hey Arianna," I look up to see Samuel making his way towards us. "Hanna," he nods his head to her.

"Samuel." She smiles at him.

"Hi Samuel, nice sweater," I tell him. He's wearing a Shrek Christmas sweater.

"Same to you," he smiles, looking at the Will Ferrell sweater I'm wearing. "How long have you guys been here?"

"We just got here, we're searching for the kitchen," I answered.

He nods his head in a direction, "Allow me to be your guide."

He starts walking off, and Hanna and I begin laughing while we follow him to the kitchen.

The kitchen was bigger than the one I have at home, it

even has a breakfast nook. The cabinets were blue with gold handles, the counters and walls are white, the floor was a light wood color. It was gorgeous.

All the snacks and drinks are laid out on the island. Bowls of chips, plates of Christmas cookies, cake pops, ice buckets filled with drinks, and there was a crockpot with a sign saying 'hot chocolate'. There was also Bacon-wrapped smokies on platers, along with dips and charcuterie boards.

"I'm going to go check out the rest of the house," Hanna tells me after she grabs herself something to drink.

"Okay, I'll catch up with you soon," I responded.

"I'm surprised that you came here."

"Why's that?" I glance at Samuel.

He walks around the island to examine the food choices. "You're not a fan of Christmas, but you have been doing a lot of Christmasy things this year." He smirks.

"Yeah, I've been sent on random holiday activities by an unknown person." I raise a brow at him, "Any chance you know anything about that?"

Samuel shrugs his shoulder while trying to hold back laughter as he eats a chip, "I have no clue what you're talking about."

"Sure, whatever you say, Sam," I playfully roll my eyes. I walk over to the crockpot and grab one of the festive paper cups for hot beverages. "Do you know if they have peppermint mocha creamer? I like putting it in the hot chocolate."

"I'll check the fridge, I'm sure Derek's mom

won't notice if you use a bit of it." He walks over to the fridge and searches through it. "Found it!"

"Yay!" I take it from him once he brings it to me. I pour a little bit into my cup and stir it into the hot chocolate. I look through my bag and grab my camera. "Do you mind taking a picture?" I ask him.

"Sure," He takes the camera and takes a picture of me drinking my hot chocolate but instead of giving the camera back, he stands next to me and makes a funny face before snapping another. "Enjoy the party, Arianna." He hands me the camera before disappearing out of the kitchen.

December 22nd

Last night was amazing. I got to see some classmates and enjoy the party. We had a contest to see who had the best ugly sweater and a guy named Jesse won. He had a drunk Santa sweater. There was karaoke and beer pong that was turned into egg nog pong. Hanna, Kate, and I didn't make it back till almost midnight. Luckily, my mother didn't mind the late return since I was attending a Christmas party that my admirer sent me to.

I'm laying back in my bed debating who my admirer could be. I was leaning toward Justin but after last night, I'm suspecting that it could be Samuel. The way he acted when I asked him about it seems suspicious, so either it's him or he knows who the person is. Three days. Three more days and I will know who my Christmas Angel is.

"Hanna, stop hogging the popcorn!" Kate reaches for the bowl.

"Shh! It's getting to the good part!" Hanna

smacks Kate's hand away.

"Hanna, we have seen this show a million times. We all know that Meredith and Derek end up together. Share the bowl of popcorn!" I laugh at the face she makes while handing Kate the bowl. It was the scene where Meredith creates a house with candles. One of the big moments in their relationship.

"You gotta be kidding me!" Hanna yells when the doorbell goes off. "Arianna, it's most likely your admirer," Hanna waves her hand at me to indicate that I should get the door.

I picked up a throw pillow and toss it at her as I went to answer the front door. I look down at our Grinch doormat and on the mat was the twenty-second card from my admirer. I picked up the red envelope and shut the door before opening it. The cover has Santa holding a bag of toys. I open it up to read today's task.

Dear Arianna,

I know you thought that I would be attending the ugly sweater party, and I was. It was nice seeing you wearing the sweater I picked out. You looked like you were having a great time. Today, you're going to be doing one of my favorite traditions. Donating toys. A lot of families struggle to provide their kids with toys for Christmas so I go shopping for toys to donate to families who need help. Target does a Toy Drive for the holiday season. Enjoy the fun, love!

Yours Truly
Christmas Angel

"Girls! We gotta go shopping! Grab your shoes and coats!" I shout after reading the card.

"So he was at the Ugly Sweater party but he didn't show up to make the cookies?" Kate questions as we walk down the toy aisles.

"Correct." I examine the shelf full of dolls looking for the princess ones. "Is this a tradition for all families?" I take one of each princess and place them into the cart.

"I don't know about everyone else but my family does," Kate assured me.

"Mine too," Hanna places some dress-up clothes into the cart.

"I'm gonna look at the boys' toys, you two go look for some little ones' toys," I tell them before pushing the cart in the direction of the boys' section.

I examine the hot-wheel cars determining which I should get and how many. I remember that Hanna's brothers collect them. Some they would play with but there were a few they kept in their packages.

"Arianna," I hear someone say as I reach to grab a red Mustang.

I turn my head to see Robbie, Hanna's oldest brother. "Robbie," I smile at him while my cheeks begin to heat up as the memory of sitting in front of him as we sled down a hill comes to mind. "What are you doing here?"

"I was about to ask you the same thing, I'm here finding last-minute gifts for my little cousins while also getting more items to donate."

"I got sent here to donate some toys," I gesture toward my cart.

"Still doing the Christmas tasks?"

"Yeah, it's actually been a lot of fun. Frustrating, but fun."

Robbie lets out a small chuckle, "Do you have any ideas who it could be?"

"A couple but now I'm more confused than ever since the person keeps throwing me off." I look at the hot wheels and nibble a little on my lower lip. "What cars would you want?"

Robbie examines the cars and takes a few off the shelf then hands them to me. I look at his choices, a Ford truck, a vintage Volkswagen, Camaro, and a vintage Mustang.

"I can help you pick out more toys if you want?" he offers.

"I would like that," a warm feeling fills me as I follow him down the aisles.

Besides the sledding, it's been a while since Robbie and I hung out. He's been so busy with college that I hardly ever get to see him. We used to hang out a lot before he graduated. Every time I was over at their place, Robbie, Hanna, and I would play games together or play pranks on their other siblings.

As we take turns picking out the toys, Robbie tells me about how busy his break from school was and how his first year of college has been. It makes me excited for my college experience to happen. Robbie's College was one of the schools I applied to since it's not far from home. The University of Cincinnati.

"I think we have enough toys," I tell him.

"Yeah, I agree. Do you want me to show you where to take them?"

"That would be a lifesaver, but I think we need to find your sister and Kate. I sent them to pick out more toys and as you can see they have not returned."

"Worse thing you could have done," Robbie laughs.

We push our carts to where the little ones' toys are located just to see Kate and Hanna playing with one of the pushing pop toys.

"Yo, it's time to go!" I shout to purposely scare them from their fun. I laughed at their reaction once they realized they got caught.

They collect the toys they have picked out and place them into the cart before we follow Robbie to where we take the toys to be donated. When we got to the location, Robbie took a picture of Kate, Hanna, and me sitting in front of our cart filled with toys to show to my admirer.

I'm starting to believe my admirer forgot about me today. It's a bit past 5 in the evening and I have yet to receive the card that holds my next task. I can barely concentrate on the book I'm reading and I'm sad thinking about not receiving anything. I'm sitting on the couch with a random show playing in the background. My mother will be home soon since she texted me saying she will be home early. Since she went in earlier. So I'm waiting patiently for her along with my card showing up.

"Arianna! Something has arrived for you!" My mom shouts as she enters the house.

I toss the blanket off me and rush to her, holding a small box with a red envelope on top.
I took the box from her and went into the kitchen to place the box on the counter. I open the envelope to see a train covered in glitter and snow on the cover. Excitement fills me as I open the card to read what my admir-

er has planned for me tonight.

My Arianna,

Nice job on all the toys you donated yesterday. I hope you love watching movies because tonight you will be watching one of my favorite movies to watch during this holiday season! Inside the box is a copy of The Polar Express along with a jar filled with hot chocolate mix, all you have to do is mix it with cups of boiling milk! Don't worry, also I provided a jar of marshmallows to top it off. I hope you like the movie. Don't forget to drink your hot chocolate ;)

Yours Truly,
Christmas Angel

Since I didn't trust myself to make the hot chocolate, I had my mom do it after we finished the chicken alfredo she made for dinner. I watch her carefully fill each mug before I put some marshmallows on top of them. We pick up our mugs and carefully walk into the living room where I have the movie ready for us to watch along with a bowl of popcorn. Do hot chocolate and popcorn mix? Who knows, but you can't watch a movie without popcorn, it's the law.

"Have you seen this movie?" I ask my mom.

"Yes, a few times when you were little."

Meaning before my father left, I don't remember much about those years nor do I remember watching this movie so young. I do know this might bring back painful memories for my mom.

"We don't have to watch this if you don't want to," I smile softly at her.

"No, no. We're gonna sit here under this comfy blanket and enjoy this classic Christmas movie while drinking our hot chocolate." She grabs the remote and plays the movie.

I admire my mom and how hard she works to give me the best in life. I'm thankful that we get to create these memories together to look back on. This holiday season has been one to remember. Right when the movie gets to the boy finding the bell under the tree, I took a picture with my mom showing the movie behind us but instead of one, I took two just to have one to keep.

December 24th

Last night was special. Something I'll never forget and I hope it'll happen every year. A new tradition for my mother and me. After the Polar Express, my mother and I stood up to watch more Christmas movies. Classics like The Christmas Carol along with How The Grinch Stole Christmas. Laughing, eating popcorn, and drinking our hot chocolate until we fell asleep on the couch.

Sadly, she had to go to work this morning and we couldn't continue the fun together. Kate and Hanna are spending Christmas Eve with their family, which means I'm spending it by myself like I do every year. The only difference is that I'm watching Hallmark Christmas movies instead of binging one of my favorite shows.

Even though there are Christmas decorations surrounding me, I feel like something is missing. Just doesn't feel like Christmas, right now. The past 23 days have been magical and today it seems like that magic has vanished.

I toss the blanket off of me as I hear a knock on the door. I don't bother rushing since I know it's my card of the day. The final card before my admirer is revealed. I open the door and reach down to pick up the velvet envelope before closing the door. I make my way into the kitchen to open the envelope to see the card that has a Christmas tree with a plate of cookies underneath.

Beautiful Arianna,

My love, it's Christmas Eve. The most important day of the year. The busiest day of the year for good ole Saint Nicholas. Which means he needs a yummy treat for all his hard work. Meaning, you have to make Santa a plate of cookies with a glass of milk. Have fun ;). Don't forget, tomorrow is the big day!

Yours Truly,
Christmas Angel

"What kind of cookies do you want to bake?" My mother asks me. I waited until she got off work so she could help me make the cookies.

"I don't know, basic chocolate chips?"

My mom walks over to the baking cabinet, examining what she has. "You're in luck, we have enough chocolate chips to make them." She starts placing random ingredients on the counter. Vanilla extract, baking soda, salt, and brown sugar along with the chocolate chips. "Get a stick of butter and eggs out of the fridge," she tells me while placing the small bag of sugar on the counter.

I make my way to the fridge to gather the items she asks for and set them down next to her mixer. "Now what?"

"Unwrap the butter and cut it into small cubes, it helps make it easier to blend."

I take a butter knife out of the silverware drawer and cut the butter up as she told me to. She takes the butter and places it into the bowl with the sugar to make it creamy. My eyes watch each action she does to make the cookie dough.

"Can you make sure the oven is preheated to 350?" She glances at me.

I go to the stove where the baking sheet is ready for the balls of cookie dough, to see the oven is indeed preheated to the correct temperature.

"Yes, it's preheated," I told her.

"Good, get the cookie scoop and place 12 balls of dough on the pan. 4 across and 3 down." She instructs me. "After you place the pan into the oven, set a timer for 12 minutes."

I place the last batch of cookies onto the plate while munching on one of them. "These are good, Mom."

"Thank you, your granny taught me how to make them."

One of the lucky things about my mother was being able to grow up learning how to bake. That's a big thing in her family. I never got to experience that, I had to learn on my own by looking up recipes on Pinterest.

"We should do this more often," She tells me.

"Do what?" I look over at her.

"Bake together."

I take the plate of cookies and set them in front of her. "That would be fun." I smile softly.

She takes a bite from one of the cookies, "These are good. Better place some of them by the tree along with milk, for Santa," She winks at me, making me laugh.

"I will."

"Goodnight, sweetie," She walks over to hug me.

"Goodnight."

Tomorrow is the big day.

December 25th

I toss my blankets off of me and rush out of my room when my alarm goes off. Why did I set an alarm? Because today is Christmas day, meaning that today I find out who's behind the cards. I climb down the stairs fast but safely since I don't want to bust my butt. Once I hit the final step, I examine the area but there was nothing. I don't even know what I was hoping to find, it's too early for someone to be standing here to surprise me. Heck, the cards even arrive later in the day as well.

I walk over to the living room, deciding to wait for my mom to wake up so we can open the gifts we got each other. As I get to the couch, I notice the plate of cookies was gone. The cookies are now replaced with a familiar red envelope.

How did my admirer get into my house?

I walk over to the plate and it's not an envelope, it's a folded red piece of paper. I'm kind of disappointed that it was a Christmas card.

Was all that was written in the note. "Where it all began," I whisper to myself, confused about what that meant. Did my admirer want me to go where the adventure all began? I grab my keys that were hanging by the front door and went straight to my vehicle to drive to the school.

I pull up to the school and went to the doors near the gym. I pull on the door and was surprised that they were unlocked. I figured since school isn't in session that they would keep the doors locked. What a way of making me feel safe. Thanks, school.

As I'm walking the halls, I'm trying to remember where exactly I received my first card. One part believes it was in the library and I stumbled upon it in my bag but another part believes it was in my locker. I repeatedly tap the note on my hand, trying to decide on which destination I should check first. My locker. I take the hall where my locker is located. If it's not there, at least I'll know it's in the library.

There it is, hanging on my door another red note waiting for me to read. I'm surprised that this time, my admirer didn't put it inside my locker. I gently peel it off my locker so it doesn't tear.

Where you had the best hot chocolate that was ever made.

I close my eyes, trying to think of the cute cafe I remember they sent me to. It was super festive and I didn't appreciate it the way that I should have.

"Holly Noelle's Sweet Cafe."

The snow crunches underneath my tires as I pull up to the cafe. I only see one other vehicle here, and the cafe lights are on. I got out and made my way to the entrance to see a woman standing behind the entrance door. She's wearing an elf outfit and holding a cup in their hand.

"Hello," I smile softly at her.

"You must be Arianna," She said to me. "These are for you." She hands me the cup along with a red note. "The cup is filled with hot chocolate."

"Thank you." I took the items from her.

I walk over to a table to set the hot chocolate down to read the note.

Maybe you'll remember this location

Below was an address that looks familiar to me but I can't remember where it leads to.

I slowly pull up in front of the house that Siri tells me was my destination. I stare at the house decorated in Christmas decorations trying to figure out why it was so familiar to me. I get out of my vehicle and walk up to the porch to knock on the front door.

A little boy opens the door, smiling brightly up at me. "Arie!" His voice holds so much excitement in it. He's the boy I bought gifts for.

"Hi," I bend down to his level. He comes up to me and hugs me. "How is your Christmas?"

"Amazing! I got so many toys!"

My heart warms knowing that I'm one of the reasons why he's having an incredible Christmas. "That's great!"

"Santa left you something here, I think he mistaken where you lived." He runs inside to retrieve the item, it didn't take him long since he came back outside in probably less than a minute.

"Thank you," I took the red note from him.

Go see what Santa left for you

I rush back to my vehicle and safely hurry back home.

My mother's vehicle is the only car that is parked at the house. My heart beats fast as I make my way up to our front door. I'm scared to know what's behind the closed door but at the same time, I'm anxious to know. Is there just another red note waiting to send me to another location? Has my admirer been my mother this whole time? I take a deep breath and finally open the front door.

"Surprise!" A group of people shouts.

"Oh my gosh!" I place my hand over my chest in an attempt to calm my heart down.

I look around the scene in front of me. Kate and Hanna were here, along with all the guys on my suspect list and my mother. They're wearing festive hats and holiday sweaters, smiling big. I'm waiting patiently for someone to come forward but no one does.

"So, who is it?" I ask them.

Silence, no one responds, they just look between themselves not saying a word.

"Come on guys, who was behind all of this?" I desperately want to know.

Hanna walks forward and hands me a red note, not saying a single word then returns to stand next to Kate.

There was this girl, who I grew to admirer
Her beauty, her strength, and her laughter
Each year, in December I begin to notice
There's never been a tree
Nor lights nor the holiday spirit
In the house, I annually visited
She never accepted gifts
Listen to Christmas music
So this year, I had a mission
To make the girl I grew to cherish

"Okay, for real. Who is it?" My eyes teared up from the handwritten note. Before anyone could respond, there was a knock on the door. I open the door to see Robbie standing there with a binder in his hands wrapped in a bow.

"Merry Christmas, Arianna." He hands me the binder that holds a note on top.

From your Christmas Angel

"It's you?" I look up at him in awe.

"Open it." He instructs me.

I flip open the binder that turns out to be a photo album. Each page holds the polaroids I took every single day this month of all the memories I created. My eyes get glossy, I can't believe he did this for me. I set the album aside and ran up to him. Wrapping my arms around his neck. Robbie immediately hugs me back.

"Thank you," I whisper to him.

"You're welcome, love."

I pull back and place a kiss on his lips. "Thank you for bringing the Christmas spirit back into my home."

This will forever be my favorite Christmas.

Epilogue
New Years Eve

Here we are, celebrating that this year has finally come to an end and what the future has to hold. Reminiscing what this year has brought to us. The bad, the good, and the challenges we had to face to mold us into who we are today. For most of us dancing around, having the time of our life, we're celebrating that in a few months, we will be graduating.

All the hard work we have been working on these past 4 years is about to pay off. At least for most of us but I know it will be for me. I've been working hard to make sure my GPA is at its highest, doing volunteer work that colleges will look for, and researching all the colleges that I want to apply to in February when the time arrives. One of them is the college that Robbie attends.

I look up at the man who is holding my hand. Robbie, the man who made my Christmas spirit come back to life. He created the most amazing adventure that sent me to do crazy tasks without revealing a single thing about himself. While also getting all my friends and my mom in on it. I don't know how they did it or how they were able to keep it a secret for so long. Especially Hanna. He's her big brother, there is no way I could manage to hide that from my best friend.

"Everyone! The countdown is starting!"

We all rush into the living room, chanting down with the TV. Some are looking around for their significant other prepping for the traditional New Year's kiss. I smile brightly at Robbie, thinking about how crazy it is that my middle crush is now my boyfriend.

"One!"

Robbie leans down and softly places his lips on mine. He pulls me into him, wrapping his arms around me and molding our lips together. He smiles at me as he rests his head against mine.

"Happy New Years," he whispers to me.

I rest my hands on the back of his next, "Happy New Year." I comb my fingers through his hair, "Better start preparing for next Christmas because there's no way you can top last year." I wink at him.

"Trust me, babe. I will be topping last Christmas." He lets out a small chuckle before kissing me again. "So be ready."

Excitement fills me. I'm anxious to know what he has planned in 334 days.

ACKNOWLEDGMENTS

Lani, my long lost sister. Thank you for helping create this story and picking the name of the main character. It's basically your fun little story.

Mom, I hope you enjoy this fun little Christmas story. Every year you put so much effort keeping the Christmas spirit alive no matter how much pain the holiday season holds for us.

My beta readers, thank you for your amazing feedback and telling me how much you enjoy reading each chapter. I loved your guys' reaction in trying to figure out who the admirer was and how shocked you were when the final reveal happened. You guys' made the adventure so fun!

Kyla Designs, thank you so much for designing the amazing cover. I had so much fun with you during the whole creating process. You're so talented and brought my vision to life. You're such an amazing person. I can't wait to work more with you in the future.

My readers, thank you for taking time out of your day and reading my creations. It brings me joy and motivation to continue writing more stories for you all to enjoy.

Stay Connected With Me

Twitter: @audrealife
Instagram: audreaslife - authoraudreacraig
audreacraig.com